THE PERFECT MISTAKE

TONI BLAKE

To Robin—
my best friend since the seventh grade
my companion and confidante
my almost sister

Dear Reader,

This book was originally written and published by Harlequin Temptation in the early 2000s. Like other early books I've released new editions of, it's been enlightening to revisit this work from so much earlier in my career and to see that it's not a book I could have written now. In these earlier works, I find a youthfulness and innocence that came from my more limited worldview at the time. I'm a very different person and writer than I was then, and it's interesting and invigorating to get reacquainted with my younger writing self.

Also worth noting: Technology plays a significant role in the story, and as we all know, technology changes fast these days. And so in re-releasing this lovely new edition of the book, I've chosen not to update it to reflect current technology, not only because it would change the story itself but because quickly enough, what's current now will again be outdated.

I hope you enjoy The Perfect Mistake!

Toni Blake

Chapter One

---

*Meet me tonight. Ten o'clock. Corner of Fourth and Walnut.
And be ready for anything.*

Penny

PENNY HALLORAN RELEASED A NERVOUS SIGH AS SHE
peered down at the note she'd just penned on a plain white
card bearing her business's logo. She wished she'd had
something more romantic to write on, perhaps scented
stationery, something with flowers or hearts. Or maybe
something sexier than that—animal print came to mind,
then leather, then lace—but where did a girl get leather
stationery? She read the words once more and wrinkled up
her nose. What she'd written them on was irrelevant. What
mattered was: Could she go through with this?

She wasn't usually an impulsive woman, and if this
could wait, she'd let it. This was the sort of thing that
needed weeks of planning to make sure it came off without

a hitch. Even the note seemed lackluster; she wished she'd had time to think of something more clever, playful. But it *couldn't* wait—Martin was going out of town tomorrow, and when he returned in a week, he expected an answer to his marriage proposal. Tonight was the night for action.

Swallowing her fears, she reached for a stapler and attached the card to the bag containing Martin's sandwich —ham and Swiss on rye, light mayo—the same as he ordered every day. Gathering the bag lunches to be delivered to Schuster Software Systems upstairs, she yelled, "Be back in five," to her sister, Patti, who stood working the bar of the Two Sisters Restaurant and Pub as the lunch hour started. Exiting the door of the restaurant that led into the skyscraper's lobby, she headed for the elevator.

This is really quite simple, she lectured herself as the elevator climbed toward the eighth floor of the downtown Cincinnati office building. *I'm just going to seduce him, that's all. Nothing to be nervous about. Men love this sort of thing*, or so she'd heard. *Martin will love it, too.* And as for why her heart was beating ninety miles an hour and her stomach felt as if it had been left back on the ground floor…well, that was only because she'd never seduced a man before. And maybe it was also because Martin's expressions of affection so far had been…less than enthusiastic. Goodnight kisses at the door that often felt more obligatory than passionate. And handholding. Martin was big on handholding. But nothing more.

Oddly, that hadn't bothered her in the three months they'd been dating. Martin was everything she wanted in a man—ambitious, dependable, sensible, and smart. Tall and lean with trim brown hair that never touched his collar, he was even somewhat handsome in a simple yet classic way. On top of that, he owned his own company, so they shared an entrepreneurial spirit, too. And at twenty-eight, she was mature enough to know there was more to life than sex. She enjoyed his companionship; they liked the same movies and had the same taste in restaurants, and they enjoyed spending lazy weekend afternoons picnicking at Eden Park, then meandering through the art museum afterward.

A few days ago, however, Martin had taken her hand in his to say, "Penny, I'm in my thirties now, and I want children before I'm too old to enjoy them. I think you and I make a good team. Will you marry me?" It had been an unexpected turn of events, all things considered. And although it hadn't been the most romantic proposal in the world, she couldn't deny that he was right. They made a good team; they were well suited.

But wasn't marriage supposed to be more than that— more than teamwork and suitability? The fact was, though, that while not the only facet of a relationship, sex *was* important. Up to now, she'd supposed it would develop between them over time; she'd decided maybe he was just a slow mover, and there was nothing wrong with that. But with a marriage proposal on the table, she just didn't think she could accept without…taking a test drive.

In fact, in the three long days since Martin's proposal, she'd done a lot of long, hard and rather *disturbing* thinking about herself. Disturbing because, not only did sex matter to her, and not only did it suddenly matter a lot, it was also beginning to matter in ways she'd never even imagined before.

After several stops to let other passengers on and off, the elevator finally opened on a crisp, contemporary lobby. Grace, the receptionist, sat behind her round desk with a phone receiver tucked beneath her chin, saying, "Mmm hmm…mmm hmm…" She shoved back a lock of wispy red hair that had fallen from the bun at her nape and rolled her eyes at Penny from behind her small, gold-framed glasses as if to say the person on the phone wouldn't shut up.

"I'll just go on back," Penny whispered, pointing. Then she padded toward the hallway that led to the private offices, her heart rising to her throat. She was about to do this, about to deliver this crazy, demanding note to sensible, *un*demanding Martin, who would likely think she was off her rocker the moment he saw it.

*But don't think like that. You've got to do this. And maybe he'll even like it. Maybe it will even…*unleash *the animal hidden inside him.* If there *was* an animal hidden inside him. *Oh please, please let there be an animal hidden inside him. Even if it's just a little one.*

Because the startling fact Penny had figured out about herself over the past few days was that an animal lurked inside *her.* She'd never known that about herself before. And okay, maybe it was a slightly timid animal at this point. Yet when she'd realized she might soon commit herself to one man for the rest of her life, it had dawned on her that not only did she have sexual desires that were going unfulfilled, but they were sort of *wild* sexual desires. Dating a guy without passion…that was okay. But when she imagined getting *married*, the package came with great sex.

Maybe she'd always just been waiting, assuming that that part of her life—a true, possibly even hedonistic sexual awakening—would come along later, that she'd meet some perfect man who would set all her inhibitions free and lead her through the thrilling, reckless affair of a lifetime…

But it hadn't happened yet, and if it was going to happen with Martin, she would clearly have to give him a push in the right direction. *It'll be worth it in the end.* She

4

made the promise to herself as she stuck her head into his corner office to find it blessedly empty. *It'll be worth it tonight when you sweep him off his feet and* he *loves it and* you *love it and a whole new sexual landscape unfurls before you both.* Actually, just thinking of the plan she'd formulated this morning was enough to leave her mildly aroused and imbued with a sudden sexy new nip of confidence. *Oh yes, this was going to be good. This was going to be* very *good.*

Her heart now pumped with more excitement than fear as she lowered the bag onto his desk in the middle of the scattered papers and folders. Her little surprise would be the perfect thing to take his mind off business, and it would be a wonderful, even generous way to send him off to his software conference in Las Vegas.

After turning the note toward the desk chair where he'd see it first thing upon sitting down, she pivoted and scurried from the room. Then she went about the business of distributing the rest of the sandwiches to the appointed offices, finishing with the new guy, Ryan. He didn't have a nameplate outside his door yet, but had been occupying the tiny office next to the conference room for the past week.

Heading back toward the elevator, she re-immersed herself in thoughts of the night to come. When she returned to the restaurant, she needed to call the limo service, then break it to Patti that she was leaving early to shop for something special to wear.

She jerked to a stop just before barreling head on into the dark suit and bright tie that suddenly loomed before her. "Oh!" She lifted her eyes, expecting to find Martin but relieved to see that it was only Ryan, who was taller and considerably broader than she'd realized before. "Hi."

"Hi," he replied, although his smile looked a little off-kilter, questioning, and it didn't take a genius to figure out why—Penny probably looked as nervous as if she'd just made off with the petty cash drawer.

"I, uh, was just…" *Preparing to ravish your boss.* This seemed like a good time to shut up rather than explain. "Enjoy your lunch," she said instead, then skirted past him toward the elevators without sparing him another thought.

She had more important things on her mind, after all. She had a seduction to orchestrate.

AFTER GRABBING a soda from the machine in the breakroom, Ryan Pierce slid into the big leather chair in his new boss's corner office, ready to get back to work. He wasn't sorry Martin had left town a day earlier than planned; it meant a quiet first Friday on the job, and it gave him a lot more space to spread out, not to mention a much better view.

Martin had suggested Ryan study some of the premiere software applications the company had created over the past few years, used to showcase their wares to potential clients. Only Ryan's computer hadn't arrived yet, leaving Ryan to work from his personal laptop, so Martin had offered up *his* computer for viewing the programs while he was away. He'd also asked Ryan to keep a check on his e-mail; if anything came in that sounded urgent, Ryan could make sure someone dealt with it in case Martin didn't see it right away.

Forcing his gaze from the bright, sunny downtown streets, Ryan spun the chair toward the desk where Penny the Sandwich Girl, as he thought of her, had left his lunch. Reaching toward the brown bag that bore the same Two Sisters logo on it as the baseball cap she always wore, he noticed something extra today—a company card stapled to the top of the bag.

As he read it, he's jaw dropped.

She wanted him to meet her? Tonight? And she wanted him to be ready for *anything*?

He was a sharp guy and it generally took a lot to baffle him, but at this, he literally reached up to scratch his head. Then he read the note again. And ripped into the sandwich bag.

Unwrapping the sandwich, he flipped through it like one might a stack of papers to confirm that *he* had the right sandwich and *she* had the right guy. Sure enough, ham and Swiss on rye with mayo. This was too weird.

After a moment's contemplation, however, he concluded that this must be her slightly offbeat way of asking him on a date. It was an unusual approach, to say the least, but maybe she was just too nervous to ask in person. Come to think of it, she'd *seemed* pretty nervous when he'd passed her in the hallway a few minutes ago, and now he knew why. She'd just dropped an invitation sandwich on his desk. And he'd noticed that she was sort of chummy with Grace, who must've told her he was working in Martin's office today.

Leaning back in the large chair, Ryan couldn't help feeling just a little arrogant. Less than a week in a new city and a cute girl had already asked him out. And she *was* cute. He'd noticed the delicate face and big blue eyes underneath that ball cap, not to mention the pretty swath of long, sandy blond hair cascading through the hat's back opening. She generally wore a loose T-shirt and shorts, so he hadn't exactly gotten a look at her shape, but he knew she had nice legs. And appearance aside, she was friendly, too, always ready with an easy smile, and he'd heard her giggling good-naturedly with Grace more than once as they'd stood chatting in the lobby.

Granted, they'd never actually shared a one-on-one conversation other than the awkward enjoy-your-lunch exchange just a minute ago, but suddenly that "enjoy your lunch" had taken on new meaning. Maybe her friendly smiles were more than friendly. Maybe her easy hellos were attempts at flirtation, only he'd had his head buried too deeply in his new job to notice.

And if any other girl had tossed a line like "be ready for anything" at him, Ryan might've backed off. He'd just moved here from Chicago to get a new start, and part of that meant settling down, walking the straight and narrow, and avoiding *anything* that might get him into trouble. But Penny the Sandwich Girl seemed...harmless. Too cute to be wild. And the way he saw it, that made her the perfect girl for him. New city, new job, and now a nice, down-to-earth girl to date.

So, sure, he'd meet her tonight. Ten o'clock. Corner of Fourth and Walnut. And though he might not be ready for anything, he would go prepared for a nice, fun, uncomplicated evening with a nice, fun, uncomplicated girl.

———

As THE LUNCH rush waned and the restaurant began to empty, Penny called Patti over to the long, mahogany bar where she was removing half-filled glasses and dirty plates to a tub bound for the dishwasher.

"Whatcha need?" Patti approached the bar clutching a damp rag in her fist.

And Penny widened her eyes as if to say *pleeeeease.* "An afternoon off. *This* afternoon, in fact. Do you mind if I leave after we get the lunch mess under control?"

Patti tilted her head, her long, light brown hair falling over one shoulder. "What for?"

"Well, you know Martin's going out of town tomorrow, right? So I want to plan a...special evening with him before he goes. Before I make my decision."

Patti's eyebrows lifted critically. "Pen, you can't seriously be thinking of marrying him. I mean, are you? Really?"

Penny pursed her lips in irritation. "Yes, I am. Really." Most of the time, she accepted her older sister's well-meaning wisdom, but at the moment, she felt uncharacteristically bold. "What of it?"

Patti blinked. "Touchy."

"Well, you would be, too, if I said something like that to you."

"I'm sorry," Patti said. "But I'm worried about this decision of yours. You haven't known the guy long enough to be marrying him."

"I've known him for two years!"

"He's been a *customer* for two years. That's not the same as knowing him."

"Even so, we get along great, we like the same things, we respect each other's ambitions, and he's a really nice person. So what if I haven't been dating him forever? If something works, it works. Right?"

Patti narrowed her gaze on Penny. "Don't take this the wrong way," she said softly, "but don't you think Martin is just a little...boring?"

Penny sighed, for more reasons than she could easily name. When it came right down to it, wasn't she really pretty boring herself? Oh, she was fairly witty on her good days and she got along well with people, but it wasn't as if she was the life of every party. In fact, Patti's accusation seemed as good an argument as any *in favor* of marrying Martin.

And she also guessed it hurt a little to have her sister cast aspersions on a man she liked and cared for. She felt the need to defend him, both for his sake and hers. "Maybe he's not as boring as you think."

"Oh?" Patti lifted her eyebrows.

And Penny said with a coy grin, "Ask me tomorrow."

"Ah." Patti nodded knowingly. "You haven't slept with him yet."

Penny chose not to answer, but suspected the warmth climbing her cheeks replied *for* her.

"Well then, by all means, take the rest of the day off. There are enough servers on the clock to keep things under control, and if the guy's leaving tomorrow, I certainly don't want to prevent the big event from taking place."

"Thanks," Penny said quietly, although she couldn't help feeling the unspoken part of her sister's words, as well —*I don't want to prevent you from finding out he's boring in bed, too.*

On every other level—family, friends, the successful business they'd built together—she and Patti usually saw eye to eye and treated each other like equals. But when it came to guys, romance, love, Penny always felt as if she were behind in the game, as if Patti knew more than her. She didn't understand why, since they'd both had their fair share of relationships, and they both remained relatively confident, content, single women. But maybe Patti had always been just a little more adventurous, a little more knowledgeable about sex, a little more…everything.

Well, Penny hoped her sister was wrong about *this*. She hoped that by the time the sun rose tomorrow morning, she'd be able to announce that Martin was indeed *not* boring, and that they were fabulously, wildly compatible in bed. *Take that, Patti.*

And it really would happen, too; she could just feel it. Everything was going to go her way. And Patti would probably drop over in a dead faint if she knew some of the stuff —*fantasies*—that had played through Penny's mind lately. She hardly knew where they were coming from, but if someone as straight-laced as she was had a secret side, then surely Martin did, too. Now, to find it.

As she made the phone call to secure a limousine, then grabbed up her purse to set out shopping, she put more of tonight's plan in place in her head. She'd figured if she was going to go through with this seduction business, she might as well go all the way. So she'd sifted through her growing sexual desires and picked out an easily realized fantasy— one of several that'd always been a loosely formed thought, yet which had gathered into something more solid in her mind over the past days.

Stepping out into the hot summer sun that beat down on the city sidewalk, she glanced at the large digital clock jutting from the corner of the building. It was almost two. T minus eight hours and her fantasy would begin, and Martin would get the thrill of his life.

———

SEVEN AND A HALF HOURS LATER, Penny sat behind the black limousine's tinted windows, feeling like someone else. Which stood to reason, since she'd paused before the mirror in her foyer not long ago trying to figure out who she saw there. With hair volumized by electric rollers that hadn't seen the light of day since high school, and eye shadow, mascara and lipstick that significantly changed the appearance of her face, and especially with the little black dress and strappy heels she wore—no wonder she couldn't recognize herself.

She'd instructed the driver to stop at the corner of Fourth and Walnut at precisely ten o'clock where a gentleman would be joining her. Only now, as she rode in unnerving silence, did she begin to wonder if the stoic thirty-something man behind the wheel suspected what was about to happen back here. So she pressed the button that raised a dark panel between them.

Eyeing the bottle of champagne in the ice bucket, she reached for it. She'd intended to save it for Martin and seduction, but she needed it now. Hopefully it would calm her down. Filling one of the long, fluted glasses provided, she drained it by half, then paused as the bubbly, tingling sensation skittered through her.

Drinking another quick glass and a half as they neared downtown, she thought she was almost relaxed. But then, maybe *relaxed* was the wrong word. Like earlier in Martin's office, fear was beginning to give way to anticipation.

Her fantasy was to have wild sex in a moving limousine. It was fairly simple as fantasies went, she supposed, but that made it attainable, too, and something about it just sounded so *glamorous* and *urgent*. Although she'd never experienced it, she'd always been fascinated by the idea of two people so truly impassioned that they couldn't wait to get home.

The limo tooled around the downtown streets, moving past Fountain Square, turning right onto Walnut, soon passing the awning-covered entrance to the Two Sisters Pub, still open for business on a Friday night. But Penny's thoughts had nothing to do with work—instead she pondered the black push-up bra and thong beneath her dress. No one who knew her would believe she even owned such things, let alone wore them. Oh, she'd always liked pretty lingerie, but the stuff she had on tonight, underneath *and* on top, fell into a different category. Even *she* could scarcely believe that good girl Penny Halloran could be this utterly wild. She bit her lip and silently thanked God for inventing champagne.

Yet as she gazed out the tinted windows as they circled the block, she suffered a startling thought. What if somehow the windows weren't really tinted well enough? What if somehow people on the street or in other cars could actually see in? She knew it was a crazy thought, but the idea of being seen was almost enough to squelch the delicious bit of naughtiness that had begun to bite pleasantly into her spine. She wanted to be wild, she wanted to give herself over to complete abandon, she wanted to be *everything* for the man she was about to seduce—but that didn't go so far as putting them on display. She wanted to shut out the rest of the world, make sure they both knew they were the only two people involved.

So she reached up and drew the tiny shade over the window next to her, snapping it shut at the bottom, then moved about the whole interior of the limo, darkening every window the same way.

When she was done, the inside of the car was as black as a cave. Maybe Martin wouldn't be able to see her well— her voluminous hair, her crimson lips, her sexy, clinging dress. But at least he would be able to *feel* that part, then peel it off her, so maybe that was all that mattered. Their hands, their bodies—all exploring and connecting. And of course, if she really *did* want him to see her, she could easily flip on the overhead light…

But maybe, she decided, this whole thing would be easier to accomplish in the dark.

With that in mind, she reached up to the car's ceiling and located the switch that controlled the interior light. Shifting it until the overhead bulb came on, she studied the settings: On, Off, and Door. She moved the switch to Off, immersing herself in a darkness that wouldn't be interrupted when the door opened.

The truth was, an old nemesis had begun to return over the last few minutes. Fear, nervousness. She'd never done anything so completely contrary to her normal self, and at the moment—champagne or no champagne—she was growing uncertain if she could pull this off without feeling like an idiot. What on earth would Martin think? What if he didn't like it? What if he thought this was too tawdry? What had she been thinking to rent a limousine just for the purpose of having sex in it?

She was a heartbeat away from forgetting the whole idea of seduction, and instead trying to convince him she'd intended nothing more than a fun evening of champagne and barhopping in Over-the-Rhine, when the limo pulled to the curb, gliding to a slow stop.

They were at Fourth and Walnut; she knew it in her bones.

And somehow, just arriving there, just knowing she metaphorically stood on the very brink of either embracing her desires or running from them, girded her strength in a way she hadn't expected.

She swallowed back her jitters, determined to take this bold leap into sexual abandon without looking back. This was it, the beginning of something wild.

———

As Ryan pushed through the revolving brass doors that led out to Walnut Street, the sultry summer air hit him like a brick. He thought to reach up and loosen his tie, but instead tightened it a little instead, wanting to look good for his date, or at least as good as a guy could look after working fourteen straight hours. It had seemed silly to drive home, then come back to meet Penny the Sandwich Girl, when there was plenty he could do at the office. He intended to make a good impression on Martin and go places in this company, so he figured there was no time to start like the present.

The glow of streetlamps lit the city night, but when he glanced around the four corners of the intersecting streets she'd indicated on her note, no one was there.

Well, no one but whoever sat in that shiny black limo. A matching black-clad driver stood at the car's door.

Ryan shifted his gaze to the green awning bearing the familiar Two Sisters logo—a cartoonish line drawing of two women, one holding up a hamburger, the other a mug of beer—and wondered if Penny might be inside. But no, she'd said the corner, so he'd wait there for a few minutes before looking elsewhere.

When he checked his watch at five after ten, he glanced up to see that the limo still lingered. And only then did it dawn on him—could *she* possibly be inside it?

Nah, surely not. Not Penny the Sandwich Girl.

Yet for some reason he kept staring at the limo, and the longer he stared, the more he began to think: *maybe*. After all, the damn thing had been sitting there since he'd walked out at ten on the dot. And she wasn't anywhere else—the sidewalks in the financial district were quiet this time of night. It seemed an elaborate first date, but the idea that she was inside began to seem more likely.

Even as he took a few tentative steps toward the big, black car, though, he suddenly debated forgetting this whole thing. Because the idea of her being in the limo came with the odd sense that perhaps this "uncomplicated girl" was a little more complicated than she'd seemed. Yet something—call it curiosity, a simple Alice-in-Wonderland need to see what lay down the rabbit hole—drew him toward the car.

His heartbeat increased as he got nearer, wondering what awaited him. And even as his better judgment told him to turn around and walk away, to go get a drink somewhere by himself and then go home, curiosity bloomed into a pinch of excitement in his chest.

"I'm supposed to meet a woman here named Penny," he said to the driver.

The man responded by opening the car's door.

Ryan stepped into the cool air of the limousine and sat down, the door shutting behind him, only to realize he'd been immersed in total darkness. Rabbit hole indeed.

"Are you surprised?"

He tried to formulate an answer, at least relieved to hear that the voice *did* belong to Penny.

"Wait, don't answer that," she said as the limo pulled away from the curb. "In fact, don't say anything at all—let me do all the talking. I'm sure you find this pretty unconventional, but I just had to do it. I just wanted to do… something special, something crazy, something wild. For once in my life, I just wanted to lose all my inhibitions, so…" she paused to swallow audibly, nervously "…I hope you won't think this is awful of me. I hope it's a part of me you'll be able to…fully appreciate, since, in all honesty, it's a side of myself that I just discovered and I want to get"— her voice dropped to a provocative tone now—"*really* intimate. So just sit back, relax, and let me make you feel good."

As she'd spoken, Ryan had waited for his eyes to adjust to the darkness, but it wasn't happening. And now he sensed her drawing nearer across the dark confines of the limo until she knelt next to him in the seat. Her knees nudged his hip and her breath warmed his neck just before she lowered a soft, sexy kiss there.

He'd been trying to remain still, quiet—trying to process this—but lost both wars when her hand slid up his thigh. He leaned his head back with a tiny groan that came all the way from his gut. But he still didn't say anything, whether too startled by the whole situation or simply obeying her orders, he didn't know. And he wasn't exactly giving it close examination; he remained much busier trying to survive the shock, and immediate pleasure, that had assaulted him upon climbing into the car.

Penny drew in her breath as she pressed her palm into the crotch of his pants, making him gasp, and—oh, he was already getting hard. She bit her lip, relieved and amazed that this was working. That quickly, it was a success she could feel emanating between them, a mutual need escalating at an incredible speed.

He'd stayed blissfully silent upon her request and it'd somehow made it much easier to move close to him, begin touching him. She'd felt his quick response in the arch of his neck against her lips and, of course, in her hand. Drawn totally into the seduction now, she rose and lifted one stocking-clad knee across his lap to straddle him, the heat of his body fusing instantly with hers.

When his palms molded to her thighs, then slid smoothly up to the hem of her dress, she took another deep breath and did what suddenly came all too naturally. Covering his hands with hers, she guided them higher, *under* the dress.

As his fingers edged past the tops of her stockings, they crossed bare skin before coming to rest on her hips, and he released another small moan. She didn't know whether it was because she had so boldly invited the touch or because he'd discovered how little she wore beneath her dress; she only knew she liked it.

She ran her fingertips through his thick hair and leaned near his ear. "Are you as turned on as I am? I want to be so, so sexy for you." Her voice came out shaky—not from nervousness now, but from sheer excitement.

"Uh…"

She giggled, then moved a teasing finger to his lips. "No, shhh, don't answer. Just kiss me."

Twining her arms about his neck, she leaned in for a no-holds-barred kiss like she'd never given Martin before. Electricity spiraled through her as he returned it, fully, passionately, with an underlying power she'd not have believed he could possess. She had the sensation of him somehow holding back even as he gave her everything she wanted, needed, and she feared that if he really let go of his desire, it might actually overwhelm her.

He deepened the kiss further, pushing his tongue into her mouth, and she moaned at the hot, tender invasion. That was when his hands drifted to her bottom—bare but for the thin strip of fabric running up the center—to press her more snugly against the incredible hardness in his pants. She'd never felt anything like the fire now intensifying between them. Even as the darkened encounter stayed steamy, slow, hot, it also grew more urgent. Urgency was no longer just a part of the fantasy now—it was a pulsing reality.

She wanted to go slow, keep the *steamy* and *hot* in place, make this aching pleasure last as long as possible. Yet at the same time, she wanted to go further. She wanted to undress him.

She worked at his tie and he leaned his head back to give her better access. Then she unbuttoned his shirt, pushing it open. She ran her hands down his bare chest, exploring the broad muscles and firm planes she'd never envisioned Martin concealing beneath his business suit.

As the limo came to a slow stop, he pulled his hands out from under the dress, reaching around until she heard the zipper at her back being lowered. Oh yes, he was undressing *her* now, too. Grazing a feather-soft touch across her shoulders, he drew the bodice to her waist, and even in the dark, she felt beautiful and wild and freer than ever in her life.

His hands rose to her breasts, caressing, kneading through the lace that still covered them, his thumbs stroking across the firm, beaded peaks. And by the time the limo accelerated again, she was panting, and grinding, rubbing his chest.

He fumbled at the front of her bra.

"In the back," she breathed.

But he didn't even bother reaching behind her this time, his breath having grown as labored as hers. He found the thin straps on her shoulders and yanked them down, his hands sliding into the lace cups to take sweet possession of her breasts. "Oh yes," she murmured at the startling sensation of his touch against her bare, aching flesh. "Yes. Yes!"

But *no, no*—she had to calm down. Because she wanted to stretch out the pleasure as long as she could. She could scarcely believe she was doing this, feeling these things— yet that remained secondary to the knowledge that she wanted more of this marvelous touching, and she knew he wanted it, too.

"Do you want me to get out of this dress for you?"

He only groaned. His way of saying *please*. She felt it.

Crossing her arms to grab hold of the fabric pooled at her waist, she removed the dress over her head in one brisk, upward movement and flung it behind her. Then, running her hands over his broad shoulders, she kissed him deeply, more heat swirling between her thighs with each feverish connection of their mouths. He caressed her breasts, lightly pinching her nipples between surprisingly skilled fingertips until she feared she'd lose her mind.

Only when his hands lowered to wind around the thin elastic at her hips, however, did she understand that it was time for more. And she was ready now. *Very* ready.

She rose up on her knees before him.

Savored the sensation of having her panties lowered over her thighs, past the lace edges of her stockings.

Heard her own ragged breath as she pressed her palms against the roof for balance when the limo turned a corner. Heard the whimpers leave her throat as he held her hips, then took turns stroking both his thumbs up the center of her, one after the other, playing her like an instrument.

But just as quickly as the hot touches melted her, his hands moved once more down to her panties. "Take them off." It was the barest of whispers, the only words he'd spoken, all powerful in their brevity.

Penny backed quickly to the seat across from him and shimmied from the undies, her anticipation rising. And then something released inside her like steam in a radiator when the cap comes off, a burning need that couldn't be denied a minute longer. She didn't care about going slow anymore, she just wanted the man, *now*.

Climbing back onto his lap, she reached for his belt buckle.

He drew her close, drew her breast into his hungry mouth, forcing her to cry out and making it considerably harder to get his pants undone. But she worked vigorously anyway, her hands trapped between them, and only when she reached into the opening of his underwear did he loosen his grip, letting her lean slightly away.

Holding him in her hand, trying not to faint with the wonder of it, her voice came out raspy. "I wanted to do this all night, make it last. But I can't wait anymore."

She lowered her body down onto him and they both moaned at the blunt, intimate connection. Even in the dark, even with this man she'd never truly felt that close to before, Penny knew a union, a soul-binding bliss, she'd never experienced or even thought possible. "I...I didn't know...sex could be like this," she whispered.

His hand found the back of her head then, bringing her down for another of his heart-stopping kisses. She sank into it, into the intense and mounting pleasure as she moved on him, their bodies joined now, his pumping rhythmically up into hers. She raked her sensitive nipples against his chest, clutched at his neck, and felt the tumultuous waves gathering inside her...until they crashed over her in sweet, shattering release.

Thrashing against him, riding it out, she leaned her head back and basked in the deepest physical fulfillment she'd ever known. Yet just as her climax began to wane, he groaned beneath her and pushed her hips down as he thrust upward, again and again, soon growling his own pleasure in her ear. And wondrously, his climax coming so close on the heels of hers somehow added an extra tiny burst of sensation deep in her core, seeming to stretch her orgasm out a little longer, just when she'd thought it was over.

"Ohhh," she sighed, still caught up in the mind-blowing sensations and trying to come back down to earth. But whether she was up or down, she knew one thing for sure—the experience she'd just shared with this man had moved her so deeply, twisted her heart, soul, and body so profoundly, that it had erased all doubt. It had erased everything but the perfection that was them—together.

"Oh yes!" she cried out. "Yes! I'll marry you!"

Yet at her proclamation, the body beneath her went instantly, dreadfully still. "Wait just a minute here. Who said anything about getting married?"

And Penny's whole body went cold as her heart sank like a stone. The voice she'd just heard didn't belong to Martin.

Chapter Two

PENNY REACHED OVERHEAD AND FLIPPED ON THE LIGHT inside the limo…then screamed and flung herself to the opposite seat. Oh God, it was the guy from Martin's office, Ryan! And they'd just…they'd just…

Using one hand to yank her bra up and the other to snatch her dress from the floor and press it over her nakedness, she gaped at him, realizing he looked almost as shocked as she felt. "What did you…?" she began. "I mean, how did you…? I mean, where's *Martin*?"

He leaned forward, his eyes wide, his jaw dropping in clear disbelief. "*Where's Martin*? Somewhere in Flagstaff, I guess. What the hell does that have to do with anything?"

Martin was in Flagstaff? Arizona? Not Vegas? What in the world was he doing in Flagstaff? And in the meantime, Ryan just sat there doing nothing to cover himself, his shirt hanging open, his broad chest looking just as good as it had felt under her fingertips, and the sight of him like that wasn't helping things at all. "I thought you were him, of course," she snapped.

"*Of course?*" He sounded incredulous, and only then did it hit her.

"Oh, you're new here. Maybe you don't know..." She swallowed. "I—we—Martin and I are..." Oh, what on earth *were* they? "A couple," she finally concluded.

He gave a slight this-explains-it-all nod, saying, "Ah," simply, sharply, although Penny thought plenty still needed to be explained.

Nonetheless, she could barely let herself focus on the guy, because even unkempt and rumpled, he looked...well, way better than she'd ever noticed up in Martin's office. And also because she was naked and they'd just...they'd just...

Her eyes darted about the limo, to the ceiling, the floor, her own nudity...*dear God, how can I get this dress on if he's just going to keep sitting there staring at me?*...and occasionally flickered back to him, the man she'd just...

Finally meeting his gaze head on and trying to forget her lack of clothing, she succumbed to the overpowering urge to come completely clean with him. "Look, it's like this," she blurted, speaking quickly. "Martin asked me to marry him, but we'd never, um, had sex. So I decided to just—just do something *wild* with him, something to try and bring out the animal in him. I thought it would be fun and adventurous to live out a fantasy, and I— Oh God, I can't believe this just happened!"

By the time she finished, he was holding up his hands, saying, "Listen, you don't need to tell me all this. It's all right. You don't need to...to..."

His words made her realize what she'd done—that easily, she'd just told this guy things about herself she'd never told another human being. "But I *do* need to," she insisted anyway. "I need you to know this isn't what I intended. I mean, it is, but I was planning on it with a different guy, a guy that I…uh….*knew*, for heaven's sake. And I need you to know that I'm not, not…really what you, uh…" she glanced down at her bareness once more, "…see here before you. I'm really that girl who delivers sandwiches and wears…clothing. Usually *loose* clothing. This girl, this girl is…someone I just made up, just for tonight, and she isn't real and she isn't me, and—" A tremendous sadness washed over her, a desperation to redeem herself in his eyes. "Please don't think what you must be thinking of me! Please just forget this ever happened!"

Even as stunned as Ryan remained, at the moment it all took a back seat to the compassion he felt for her, with her eyes so glassy, her voice so frantic. He hated the panic glimmering in her pretty gaze.

There were a million things he wanted to tell her. How sexy she was, how beautiful. And that he didn't think less of her for what had just happened, but that she *must* be the woman she claimed she'd made up, because you couldn't fake that. And despite his shock and helplessness, there was no way in hell he'd ever be able to forget such outstanding sex. Instead, though, he just stayed quiet, as he had through the other, better part of their encounter, because he had a feeling she wouldn't believe or even want to hear any of the thoughts playing through his head.

"Martin is in…Flagstaff?" she finally asked.

Ryan nodded. "He left a day early; a last minute decision to see a client out there."

"But how did you end up in…?" Her voice trailed off as her head tilted in confusion.

"I got a note on my sandwich from you."

"*Martin's* sandwich."

"No, I checked, it was mine. Ham and swiss on—"

"Rye with mayo," she finished for him.

He nodded, this other piece of the picture slowly becoming clear.

"Same sandwich," she murmured.

"How's that for a coincidence," he replied lamely.

She gave her head a slight shake. "I didn't know. My sister made some of the sandwiches today."

But he was way past the sandwiches already, and feeling sheepish. "When I saw the note, I thought you were asking me out."

Across from him, she nodded, still sitting there in a bra and stockings, her dress tossed over her. His gaze kept dropping to her bare hip, to the curves so visible behind what the dress covered. He really *did* think she was beautiful and sexy, and despite himself, he could feel hints of arousal rising again already.

"I'm sorry," he said then, although he wasn't entirely sure what for. Still thinking about her body even after her heart-wrenching pleas? Or simply being arrogant enough to think she would ask him out without even knowing him, arrogant enough to approach a limousine thinking it was there for him?

Well, she'd been right about one thing—he should've been ready for anything, should've heeded that warning. A nervous quiet lingered between them and he wished he could take his eyes off her, but with a nearly naked woman sitting across from him—well, where else was he gonna look?

"I'm the one who's sorry," she finally said. "I mean, even in the dark, you'd think I'd recognize…"

He nodded, agreeing.

"But then, I just now noticed"—she gave him a timid once over—"you look like him, kind of."

He nodded again. It was true. He and Martin were about the same height, shared the same basic build, and wore their medium-brown hair in a similar style. "Yeah, kind of." Then he forced a laugh, despite the fact that nothing was very funny.

"I'm trying to let that make me feel better," she said, "like it's a mistake anyone could've made, but…" Her eyes dropped shut and she lifted her hands to cover her mouth, as if the horror of what she'd done was hitting her all over again.

His heart tightened into a tense knot and he felt the inclination to reach out and touch her knee to comfort her, but that would be the wrong move. "Listen, don't feel bad," he said instead. "I…don't think badly of you, honest."

She raised her gaze. "But I just…" She closed her eyes once more as if to shut out what had happened, then opened them wide. "Oh God, I just seduced you! I had my way with you! I didn't even give you a choice!"

He swallowed, then spoke quietly. "I had a choice."

They peered at each other in uncomfortable silence until she said, "Would you mind if I turned the light back out so I can get dressed?"

"Sure."

"And maybe you could, uh"—she motioned vaguely toward him—"zip up, too."

At this, he flinched. He'd been too caught up in what was happening to realize he still sat there unbuttoned and undone. "Um, yeah, sure thing. Sorry about that."

The return of darkness was more jarring than he'd anticipated. For a few brief seconds, he wondered what she would do if he reached out to find her in the blackness and began to kiss her again, touch her, push his way inside her again. He wondered if it wouldn't be simpler to just go back a few minutes in time, back to her thinking he was someone else and back to him thinking she wanted him, if it wouldn't be easier to just leave the lights off and pretend. But they were only fleeting thoughts that made no sense, so he tucked and buttoned until everything was back in place save for the tie hanging loose about his neck.

When the rustling of fabric and sounds of sliding zippers ceased and the overhead light illuminated the car once more, Penny pointed to a bottle of champagne jutting from an ice bucket. "Want some?"

Lifting the open bottle from the ice, Ryan noticed it was half-empty. "Looks like you got started without me."

"I needed it for courage," she admitted. "Now I just need to be drunk." Taking the bottle from his hand, she tipped it to her mouth and took a hefty swig.

"Sounds like a decent idea," he said. She passed the bottle back and he swallowed a long drink, too, then spoke uncertainly. "I guess I should, uh, tell the driver to take me to my parking garage."

Her slight hesitation made him wonder if maybe she didn't want him to go, if maybe she actually wanted to drink and commiserate together—but it was not to be. "Um, yeah," she said with a definite degree of finality.

Looking over his shoulder, he opened the panel and gave the driver directions to where he parked his car. He grew suddenly embarrassed on Penny's behalf, wondering if the guy had heard anything or if, God forbid, he'd felt any...movements.

Thankfully, though, the driver's eyes betrayed nothing, and Ryan shut the panel, leaving him and Penny awkwardly alone again. As the limo continued winding through the downtown streets, they stayed quiet, simply passing the champagne back and forth until he offered her the bottle one final time with the words, "Last drink?" She took it, emptied it, then chucked it back in the ice bucket.

She looked so...despondent. And he sort of wanted to

hug her, tell her again it was all right, but this time do it while peering into her eyes and maybe stroking her hair.

But she was practically *engaged* to his boss, for God's sake—or at least that's what he thought she'd said—and things were horrible enough already without him doing something stupid like being tender with her.

As the long black car finally glided across the echoing garage toward the only vehicle still there at this hour, he leaned forward and met her gaze. Despite this being what she wanted, and despite the fact that she belonged to his brand new boss, he felt bad leaving her after what they'd done together. "Are you gonna be all right?" he asked, and this time he *did* touch her knee.

She trembled a little—he felt it beneath his fingertips—and took a deep breath before lifting her gaze. "Um, yeah. I guess."

But when he reached for the door handle and began to step out of the car, she grabbed his wrist. He glanced back to find her eyes looking frantic again. "You won't tell Martin about this?"

Tell his boss he'd just had wild sex with his girlfriend? "Uh, no, definitely not. It'll stay just between us. Promise."

"Thank you."

Not bothering to point out that she wasn't the only one with something to lose, he exited the limo, took one last look at her sitting there wearing her sexy dress and distressed expression, then closed the door.

———

RYAN SAT down behind Martin's desk early the next morning, although even sitting in the man's chair felt intrusive now, like he was trespassing. He vowed not to think about that, though, since he'd come here to work. The office lay desolate on a Saturday morning, but it was just as well; it would help him concentrate, stay focused. All this work would get him firmly entrenched in Schuster System's operations, and it also seemed his only hope of getting his mind off what had happened last night, since hours of tossing and turning in bed hadn't done it.

He shook his head as the unsettling truth assaulted him once more. Already, this felt like another disaster in the making, another fist with a chokehold on his career. Unfortunately, this wasn't the first mistake he'd ever made.

Only two months ago, he'd lost his job at ComData in Chicago, for missing a client meeting, of all things. A missed meeting was an embarrassing *faux pas*, definitely, but he'd not have believed it could earn him a pink slip until it had happened.

It had all occurred innocently enough—he'd planned to have dinner with a woman he'd recently met, then hook up afterward with David Collins and Roger Borcherding, the top guys at Fischer International, in their hotel lounge for drinks. Ryan had been assigned to manage their system conversion and the executives had suggested touching base that evening after their flight arrived.

He'd picked up his date, Maggie, at her suburban office after work, planning to eat and return her to her car by eight thirty, but he'd been enjoying the evening so much that the first time he'd looked at his watch, it was quarter 'til nine.

Then, after hurriedly paying the bill and racing back to Maggie's car, they discovered it had been broken into. It was drivable, but the passenger side window was shattered and her stereo system ripped out.

She encouraged him to go ahead, but he'd refused to leave her there alone in the dark waiting for the police. After assuring her that staying wouldn't be a problem, he called the hotel and asked to have a message delivered to the two men waiting in the bar since he didn't have either of their cell numbers.

When he finally made it to the hotel around ten thirty, however, he discovered that not only had his message never made it to the lounge, but Collins and Borcherding were angry. He knew he'd cut it too close on time in the first place, but he'd been sure they'd understand the position he'd been in with Maggie's car, sure that any decent guy would've handled it the same way.

All *they* could see, however, was that he'd stood them up, wasted their time, and proven himself irresponsible. It had made such a bad impression that Fischer had ultimately dropped ComData and gone elsewhere for their software needs, and in the process pretty much made him out to be the devil incarnate.

He still remembered standing in Mr. Lever's office, numb, trying to absorb the unbelievable results of that night. "We can't afford these kinds of screw-ups, Ryan," Lever had said. "And we can't afford to have someone on our team who doesn't put us first. It's nothing personal, but we have to let you go."

Ryan propped his elbows on the desk in Martin's office, then began to rub his temples as he recalled the whole disaster.

The job loss had been devastating financially—he'd had a mortgage on a high-rise condo overlooking Lake Michigan and he sent money home to his elderly parents in rural Indiana every month, money they needed to make ends meet.

And the job loss had also devastated him personally, as well. He recalled the thoughts that had run through his head as he'd stood there outside the office building he'd just been escorted from. *This isn't the kind of guy I am, the kind of guy who gets fired from jobs; this isn't how things are supposed to be.* And it had happened all because he'd been having too much fun flirting with a woman to keep an eye on the clock. He didn't think he'd ever made such a bonehead move.

But then...the truth was, even before the fiasco at ComData, his social life had gotten him into trouble. He'd been the best and the brightest young system designer on his team at Futureware, also in Chicago, yet he'd also been fresh out of college and frat life. He'd lasted five years there, but too many late nights had led to too many late mornings. He'd always been the guy who came straggling into meetings long after they'd started, tie crooked, eyes bloodshot. He'd been young and stupid and careless.

That job he'd eventually chosen to leave on his own, but only after he'd been passed over for promotions numerous times. The fault was his, but he'd decided he just needed a new start. And things had been going great at ComData until that one tragic night. The job loss had been made even worse when Mr. Lever told him he couldn't in good conscious give him a reference, which made it feel pretty damn personal, no matter what the guy said. And in fact, when he'd started applying for other system design jobs, he'd discovered that news of his blunder at ComData had already made the rounds in the Windy City, and no one wanted to hire a guy who lost big accounts. He'd effectively been blackballed in his field in Chicago.

So...that left him with Cincinnati. Another new start. A smaller, more conservative city where he'd been sure he could buckle down, act responsibly, and finally reap the rewards of being damn good at his chosen profession. A fresh, young company with a solid track record. A nice condo with a river view. *And a scantily clad girl in a dark limo who'd turned out to be his new boss's fiancée.*

He buried his head in his hands a little deeper, then a few seconds later thrust himself up out of the chair. Coffee. He needed coffee.

After making his way to the coffee machine, then digging in the pocket of his blue jeans for change, he reflected on the unbelievable events of the previous evening as the hot liquid trickled into the white cup below. He'd been terribly sorry to find out she belonged to Martin, and the more he thought about it, the more it grated on him. Because the guy was his boss, and he would surely lose this job, too, if she started feeling guilty enough to tell. And also because he couldn't deny loving what had happened between them once he pushed all the weird parts of it aside.

He'd never been that swept away—dare he even think dominated—by a woman before. Not that she was rough, by any means—more sweet and sexy than rough—but she'd left him feeling thoroughly seduced, thoroughly… taken. He could still hear the tantalizing shift in her voice when it had edged from nervous and explanatory into seductive. He could still feel her soft curves, the lace of her barely there lingerie, the weight of her breasts in his hands. He could still feel the heat of her kiss, her moisture on his fingertips…

Flinching to discover he still stood in the bright light of the breakroom, he swallowed back the consuming memories and reached for his coffee. Taking a gulp, he told himself to concentrate on work and get this woman off his mind. As much as possible anyway.

Still, even as he made his way back through the lobby and down the hall to Martin's office, his thoughts dwelled on her. Specifically, on how much he'd hated finding out she'd been embarrassed by that hot, sexy side of herself, and how he wished everything were different, that there could be more between them, that he could show her how incredibly amazing that part of her was.

But it's best this way. It was crazy for him to even *wish* for something else with her. Clearly, the girl was wilder than she even understood, or last night wouldn't have happened with *anybody*. And while there was certainly nothing wrong with being a little wild, it was *not* a quality he needed in a woman right now.

What he needed right now was stability—a dependable job with a dependable income and a dependable future. What he didn't need was an affair with the boss's fiancée, or girlfriend—hell, whatever she was. His mistake at ComData had seriously screwed up his career, and getting his job at Schuster Systems had been an amazing stroke of luck, since Martin hadn't asked for references. But if he lost *this* job, how would he bounce back? He'd come here to start over and he couldn't afford another black mark next to his name.

He drained his coffee cup as he settled back behind the desk, needing that extra jolt of caffeine to get his mind off this and back onto work. Work, work, work—it was all-important, all that mattered here. And hopefully last night's escapade would fade away just like she wanted it to, like they *both* wanted it to.

Except for the memory of the sex, of course. That wouldn't fade.

Taking a deep breath, Ryan reached for the folder he'd plucked from his own closet-sized office on his way into Martin's. Martin had dropped it in his inbox before leaving, telling him it contained the specs on his first major project at Schuster, and that he'd scheduled a planning session for Ryan with the client on Monday afternoon. It was important that this first assignment go well, so it was imperative that he familiarize himself with it before the meeting two days from now.

Flipping open the folder, his gaze fell on the neatly typed job form.

Client: Two Sisters Restaurant & Pub
Contact: Penny Halloran

Oh God.

How could this be? How could fate be cruel enough to throw this woman back in his face like this?

When he finally started breathing again, his eyes dropped farther down the page to the bright yellow sticky note bearing the bold print he already recognized as Martin's.

Ryan—meet with Penny at her house on Monday, two o'clock. Grace can give you directions.

M

Penny's *house*? If this wasn't awful enough already, why on earth would they meet at her *house* of all places?

He swallowed, hard. This was bad. Really bad. Because unbidden images were already filling his brain.

He saw her in the black bra and panties he'd never really gotten a good look at but could imagine easily enough in his mind.

He saw her atop him, in his lap, grinding.

He saw her soft, delicate hand reaching down, wrapping around him. *God, yes.*

And then he saw everything in this new city, everything in this new job…going horribly, irredeemably wrong…

———

PENNY CLOSED THE PAYROLL BOOK, then locked the checks she'd just written in the desk. Patti had gone to the bank for change, the only server on duty was out running an errand, and Penny was glad to be alone in the quiet of the pub. Business was always slow on Saturday afternoon—this part of Cincinnati's downtown thriving much more during the work week—but it was a good day to get accounting and other behind-the-scenes work done.

She only came in on Saturdays if the workload was heavy or if she was bored or needed a distraction from something, and today, she *definitely* needed distraction. Besides, she was scheduled to spend a lot of time with a system designer in the coming few weeks, so it didn't hurt to get ahead. She and Patti had decided it was time to update the pub's computer systems—from the accounting program to the one used to by the servers to place orders.

When she'd finally dragged herself in the door last night, she'd found her answering machine blinking, although she'd known what she would hear even before pressing the button. "Hi Penny, it's Martin." *Here we are, considering marriage, but he doesn't even expect me to recognize his voice.* "I'm calling from Flagstaff—I left early to meet a client. I should have let you know, but it was a last minute decision, and I've been busy since the plane touched down. I'll call you after I reach Las Vegas, and of course, I'll look forward to hearing your thoughts on my proposal when I get back."

As Penny had erased the message, she'd thought it sounded more like he'd made a business proposition than a request to spend their lives together. But then, Martin was Martin. A consummate businessman, and she could respect that. And so what if he was a little...stiff?

Oh, Martin, Martin, Martin. What have I done? Despite coming to work, it was impossible not to dwell on her unwitting betrayal last night. She winced, recalling her total mortification upon discovering she'd had sex with the wrong man. And after returning home, she'd done something she hadn't done in years—cried herself to sleep.

Sadly, she wasn't sure if the worst part was seducing a guy she didn't even know...or enjoying it so darn much.

Exiting the restaurant's small office, she made her way behind the bar. As she filled a glass with soda from the spray nozzle, she considered adding a little rum, still compelled to try drinking her mistake away—but already battling a champagne headache, she resisted the temptation.

Whether she liked it or not, Ryan had helped her live out a fantasy. Her breath caught as she remembered how wickedly fun and exciting it had been. Sure, she'd thought he was Martin, but no matter *who* he was, he'd done everything *so* right. Of course, it could be argued that she'd done most of the work—but his hands, touching her...his mouth, kissing her so thoroughly...

She'd never imagined sex with a stranger could be so good. She believed that intimacy had to be there first, before sex. Somehow, though, with him, it had seemed to happen *during* the sex. To her horror, even upon finding out he wasn't Martin, she'd still felt close to him after what they'd shared.

Setting down her glass, she ran her hand across the smooth, clean bar top. Another of her loosely formed fantasies involved having sex *there*. She didn't know why. Maybe it was about doing something private in an inherently public place, or maybe it had to do with sort of privately *christening* this establishment she'd built herself—along with her sister, of course. But either way, as she stood there alone with her thoughts, she found herself envisioning it easily enough, she and Ryan passionately writhing together on the long mahogany bar. Ryan, not Martin.

But it only made sense, she reasoned as ripples of sensation snaked down her spine. She and Ryan had shared a terrible, wonderful sort of intimacy last night. And despite her regret, this man knew how to kiss a woman, how to touch a woman. This man was... She rolled her eyes. *The wrong man to be thinking about!* So she had to stop it, now. Besides, how would she ever face him again anyway?

When the pub's door opened, Penny flinched, feeling almost as if Patti could read her mind. Plunking a big leather satchel of change on the bar, her sister devilishly raised her eyebrows. "I forgot to ask earlier. *Is* he boring?"

Penny swallowed the lump that rose to her throat. "Um, no." After all, Patti had not specifically identified the 'he' in question.

At this, however, Patti appeared even more eager and interested. "Can I have details?"

Penny smiled. "No again."

And her sister frowned. "You're no fun."

"I don't think *he* would agree with you on that," Penny said, then wished she could draw the words back. *What am I doing, perpetuating this conversation and this mistaken idea of who "he" is? I must be losing my mind.*

And she knew for *certain* she'd lost her mind when she looked up to see Ryan coming in the other door, the one that led from the building's lobby, and that *couldn't* be happening, it just *couldn't*. What on earth was *he* doing here?

"Hi," he said. He looked incredibly sheepish. And incredibly handsome. How had she not noticed that before? Her skin tingled. "I was hoping you might be here."

"Hi," she replied, feeling her face pinch up at the very sight of him and knowing she must look as glad to see him as she would an IRS auditor.

Wearing faded jeans and a polo shirt that revealed just a hint of the muscles she'd felt beneath her fingers last night, he stepped up to the bar, his earnest brown gaze shining on her. "Um, I was wondering if I could talk to you alone for a minute."

They both glanced at Patti, whose pale blue eyes had grown as round as two beer mugs. "Don't mind me," she said awkwardly. "I'll just…put this change away in the office." Hefting the satchel from the bar, she gave Penny a quick last glance, then flurried into the back.

Penny nervously returned her attention to Ryan. He'd taken a stool at the bar and was leaning forward on his elbows, closer than she expected. She caught her breath, then said, "What's up?" as if they were casual friends or something.

"I just…wanted to make sure you're all right."

"Oh," she replied. *Very clever response, Penny.*

"Because last night you seemed pretty upset. I felt bad leaving you."

Oh wow, how sweet. She lifted her gaze to his and realized he'd been doing a much better job of looking her in the eye than she'd done with him so far. Still, she pulled herself together and gave what she thought a much more convincing answer than she had last evening. "I'm really fine," she lied. "I mean, I was certainly shocked." She even faked a good-natured laugh. "But there's really nothing to do other than put it behind us."

He smiled again, a big, wide, what-a-relief smile. "Good. I'm glad you feel that way—because as it turns out, you and I are going to be working together."

Her jaw dropped. "Pardon me?"

He added a shrug to his smile. "I just found out Martin assigned me the job of designing your computer system."

"Oh."

"So…is that all right with you?"

"Yeah. Sure." Of course it wasn't all right, but what would Martin think if she refused to work with Ryan? What possible reason could she give? She certainly didn't want to jeopardize the guy's job in any way. "We'll just have to…put last night behind us, like I said," she added, wondering why she was still talking about it if she was so eager to put it behind them.

"Definitely." He nodded vigorously.

"Of course." She nodded right back.

"I'm really sorry. I know this will be awkward."

"It'll be fine," she insisted, too desperately.

"Although I don't know why Martin wouldn't do the job himself, being…so close to you and everything."

She almost laughed then, considering that she'd techni-cally been much closer to Ryan now than she'd ever been to Martin, but the word *close* just stirred up too many sensual memories. "Actually, Martin doesn't do much designing anymore now that the company's grown, so I knew he was assigning it to someone else."

"And I was, uh, wondering about something else, too. Martin's instructions said we were…meeting at your house?"

She nodded some more. "I've been typing all my notes

into my computer at home, but I've suffered a series of mishaps over the last few months."

"Mishaps?"

"Well, first, my printer broke. I bought a new one, but something's wrong with the connection, because it won't print. After that, I managed to get a CD jammed in the drive. Then last week, during a thunderstorm, lightning zapped my modem."

"Wow." He looked dumbfounded by her streak of bad luck.

"So the computer still *works*," she went on, "but I don't have any way to move the information out of it. Martin has promised to get it all fixed, but he hasn't had time yet, so he suggested that rather than wait, we just work from my place." Then it occurred to her to ask, "Is that all right? I mean, will you be okay with…coming to my place?"

"Sure. Of course." He nodded.

"Okay." She felt herself nodding again, too. "Good."

"Well then," he said, pushing to his feet, "I'll, uh, look forward to getting together, talking about your needs, and trying to fulfill them." Then he cringed. "Your *system* needs, I mean."

More nodding on her part, repeatedly, almost convulsively. "Yes, right, my system needs."

"See you…then," he concluded, disappearing out the door before she could utter another word. She finally quit nodding and simply stood there, staring after him, then reached behind her for a bottle of rum. Maybe adding just a dollup to her drink wouldn't hurt anything, after all.

"Wasn't that the new guy who works for Martin?"

She looked up, this time caught in the act of spiking her own drink, as Patti peeked cautiously from the office.

"Um, yeah." She tried to sound very casual as she wiped the bottle off with a rag—dusting, she was just dusting it, that was all—and returned it to the shelf behind the bar.

"Cute," Patti said, then gave her head a suspicious tilt. "Why did he want to talk to you alone?"

Swallowing, Penny pasted on a fake smile, something this whole bizarre situation was giving her a lot of practice with. "He's going to design our computer system. Just wanted to touch base, that's all."

"But...*alone?*" Patti raised her eyebrows.

Penny just replied with a shrug. "I guess it's just because my name is listed as the main contact. Maybe he thought you were a spy or something." Then she made herself laugh, as if she'd just said something terribly witty. "Who's on the schedule to tend bar tonight?" she asked, effectively steering her sister onto another subject—since she had no intention of discussing this one any further. Or thinking about it, either.

But that part was harder. Because if she'd started to calm down at all about last night, that was over now. Her insides had resumed doing flip flops.

Partially because she felt sick about Martin and what she'd done and what Martin didn't know. And partially because she was so darned excited about seeing Ryan again.

Chapter Three

On Monday afternoon, Penny sat on the couch in her small, tidy house, nestled on a quiet Hyde Park street, waiting for Ryan to arrive and thinking about her sister's unspoken suspicions.

"So, big meeting with that cute systems guy today, huh?" Patti had asked right in the middle of the lunch rush a couple of hours ago, customers and servers navigating the pub around them.

"Uh, yeah." Again, Penny had been the queen of casual.

Not that Patti bought it. A wicked grin had graced her face. "Is there something going on between you two that I don't know about?"

"Something going on?" Penny had repeated as if it were the most preposterous accusation she'd ever heard. "I don't even know the guy."

Now, as she waited for this guy she didn't know but with whom something had definitely gone on, she asked herself why she hadn't just told Patti the truth. Even as mortifying as it was, and even if she often found herself at odds with her sister when they discussed their love lives, they'd always been honest with each other. Penny knew everything about Patti's sex life, from the moment she'd lost her virginity right up to the guy she'd slept with for the first time just last weekend, and Penny usually felt equally as compelled to confide in her sister.

This felt different, though, as if it were something so intimate she simply couldn't share it. And that had to do with more than her embarrassment over it; it had to do with…her fantasies, and with the same reason she hadn't told Patti about *them*, either. There were just certain moments that a woman wanted to keep all to herself, moments so intense that even sisters couldn't be let in. Like her fantasies, she wanted to keep her limousine encounter with Ryan entirely private, belonging to her and no one else.

Well, it belonged to him, too, of course, but guys just didn't treasure the outstanding, individual moments of their lives the same way women did, did they? No, surely not.

And then it hit her—hard.

I treasure what happened. In fact, hardly a moment had passed since Friday night that it hadn't permeated her thoughts and senses.

How the heck had that happened? How could she possibly treasure something that had taken place with a man she didn't even know? Especially when it was something that should have her quaking with guilt.

Yet again she supposed it came back to the fantasy he'd helped her live out. Which meant it really had nothing to do with *him*, exactly—only her and her fantasies, right?

Just then, the doorbell chimed. She nearly leapt from the couch as a familiar tingle ran the length of her body. She was about to see him again.

Smoothing back a lock of hair and wishing she'd worn something prettier, she walked to the door and took a deep breath, trying to prepare herself for the afternoon ahead. Because even if she tried to pretend otherwise, the truth was, this felt far from finished.

———

RYAN STOOD on the doorstep thinking about what he'd envisioned the other day upon finding out about this meeting—her, on top of him. Ludicrous. He didn't want that and neither did she. They'd had a bizarre encounter in a limo, but they were putting it behind them now like the mature young professionals they both were.

Of course, that didn't mean a little spiral of sensation didn't bite into him when she answered the door, and it didn't mean he didn't spend a fleeting thought on her black bra even when she appeared in her typical shorts and T-shirt. But he was a guy—that sort of thing ran in his blood, right? He decided that made it okay, so long as he knew where his head and heart lay, which was in being mature and doing this job without any further…intimate complications.

"Hi," he said. He found himself blinking at her uneasily. She wasn't wearing the baseball cap today and her hair fell over her shoulders in silky waves. Her dark blue eyes struck him as warm and deceivingly innocent.

"Hi." She glanced at his face, then her shoes, then his face again.

Already, they both seemed nervous. This wasn't going to work without some radical move on his part.

"Listen," he told her, stepping inside, "like I said the other day, I know this is awkward, but let's not worry about it anymore. How about this—let's just pretend this is the first time we've ever met." He held out his hand and put on a professional voice along with a professional smile. "I'm Ryan Pierce from Schuster Systems and I'll be designing the system for your restaurant."

Her sweet smile seemed appreciative. "Penny Halloran, half owner of the Two Sisters Restaurant and Pub."

She took his proffered hand, squeezing it gently in hers, after which they moved to the living room, to a desk where she'd pulled up an extra chair next to her computer. Maybe this would all be okay.

By the time she'd offered him a drink and returned with two glasses of iced tea, he'd drawn his laptop from its leather case and set it up beside her monitor. "Let's get started," he suggested, taking a seat.

"I've made a lot of lists and typed up some questions and ideas," she said, sitting down next to him. She motioned to her computer screen. "Now I only hope they make some sort of sense."

He smiled in response, still his professional smile, and it even came out sort of naturally this time. "I'm sure we can make sense of them together and transform them into a workable system for you."

To his relief, things soon settled into a nice, easy rhythm, and before long, he felt so comfortable talking business with her that it almost shocked him. Maybe he'd not really believed things could go well, but suddenly they were. Penny filled him in on all the things she wanted the system to handle, from payroll and budget to food and drink orders, and he couldn't help being impressed by how well thought out her ideas were.

"This is great," he said. "You've done half my work for me. Now let's see if we can start putting your ideas together with mine." He turned to his laptop and pulled up the first of several screens he'd already started creating from templates at the office.

"Oh, you used our logo!"

"Yeah," Ryan replied, following her eyes to his computer. He'd thought the system might feel more distinctly like it belonged to her and her sister if he headed each screen with a small graphic of the Two Sisters logo. On the opening screen, the graphic appeared much larger. "I just scanned it from the card on…" Oops, he hadn't meant to bring this up again, "…my, uh, sandwich bag the other day."

She tensed at his words, but he could see she was a trouper, trying to keep right on acting normal. "That's great. I love it." She even met his gaze for good measure, but at the moment—at his unwitting reminder of things past—he couldn't help looking into her eyes just a little more deeply than seemed prudent.

Which made her jerk her gaze back to the computer.

Good idea. He did the same.

"So this is a start-up screen?" she asked.

"Right. Or, more precisely, a home screen." Back to business. "We'll label the boxes under the logo with the various system components we create, like payroll or menu."

"Cool." She nodded.

"What I suggest we do next is go over each of the areas in detail. I'll design everything according to your specifications, then we'll go into test phase, looking for things that don't work, or changes you'd like to make. Sound good?"

"Sounds great."

The serious work began then, and after much intensive talking, brainstorming, and studying screens, he felt he'd gathered enough information to lay out preliminary designs for the accounts payable and receivable parts of the system. And when Penny leaned back in her chair next to him, he glanced toward the antique-looking clock on her mantle to see that it was already five thirty.

"Time to call it a day?" she asked.

"Well," he admitted with a grin, "I haven't exactly been following normal business hours lately, so if I knock off this early, I'll feel like I'm really slacking. I'll probably head home and get back to work, start getting some of this keyed in."

Penny gave her head a derisive tilt. "Don't tell me you're one of those guys who burns the midnight oil and never takes time to stop and smell the roses."

He shrugged. "Looks like you're onto me."

"That's bad for your health, you know. And I know your type. I bet my sandwiches are the healthiest food you've been putting into your body lately. Am I right?"

"Okay, you caught me again. I've had a standing late night date with the girl at the McDonald's drive-thru for the past week. But when you're in a competitive market and you want to get ahead, you've gotta give a hundred percent."

"Sure, but you don't have a hundred percent to give if you never stop to refuel." She shifted her gaze toward the kitchen. "Me, I'm gonna heat up some leftover pot roast. *Real* food," she added teasingly.

"Wow, pot roast." His eyes opened a little wider at the very thought. "I haven't had anything that good in ages." Though he winced inwardly as soon as he'd spoken—he hadn't meant to sound like he was hinting for an invitation.

And her reply affirmed his fears. "I have plenty. I made dinner for my parents and sister yesterday, but I'll never be able to eat the rest myself."

He shook his head. "Uh, thanks, but no. I'm really eager to get to work on this. I want to have some fresh screens to show you before we meet tomorrow afternoon." *And I also want to make sure we keep this all business.* The afternoon had gone surprisingly well and he'd hate to risk screwing it up now by changing it into something social.

"I really don't mind. I can heat it up in the microwave and toss in a couple of potatoes while I'm at it. It'll take fifteen minutes. And it's the least I can do, considering all the overtime you're planning to put in on this job. Unless…" she added, cringing slightly, "you think eating together would be too…"

"No," he said. "It's not that." A blatant lie. He definitely thought it would be too weird, awkward—maybe even tempting?—but he certainly couldn't admit it. Besides, maybe she was right; maybe he needed a little down time if he was going to keep doing worthwhile work. He'd kept his professional wits about him all afternoon, so surely he could handle another half hour or so in her presence. "Okay," he finally conceded, summoning a smile. "I'd love some real food."

When he offered to help, she assigned him the job of setting the small table in the breakfast nook that jutted off the old-fashioned red and white kitchen. "Very retro," he said appreciatively of the red Formica table, circa 1960.

"Very garage sale." She laughed as she dug in the refrigerator, which also looked like it had a few miles on it. "I like old things," she added, turning toward him, a large bowl covered with plastic wrap cradled in her arms. "I love these old hardwood floors and the old wooden cabinets. I bought this house with the idea of remodeling it, but by the time the restaurant was doing well enough that I could afford it, I'd grown attached to it all, just the way it is."

He found himself looking at her face then, seeing her features more clearly than ever before, concentrating on her perky nose, her easy smile. He smiled back. But then he stopped, because it was the smart thing to do.

He set out the aqua Fiestaware plates she'd handed him, then rummaged in her drawers until he found silverware. Before, he'd only been vaguely aware of the vintage qualities of everything in her house, but now that it had been drawn to his attention, he thought it was very Penny —simple, no-nonsense, yet full of an unnamable appeal.

Then, of course, he had to amend the thought—Penny was not as simple as he'd originally assumed. But outwardly, the parts she showed the world, and the parts he was *supposed* to see, indeed fit with the home she'd chosen. He couldn't deny feeling comfortable here.

A few minutes later, they sat down together at the table. "This is great," he said, savoring each bite of pot roast he put in his mouth. "I don't think I've had this since I lived at home."

"Really?" Her eyes widened. "I don't think I could survive without home cooking. It's hard to cook for just myself, but I try to as much as possible."

"Is that why you opened a restaurant?"

She shrugged. "Partly. But I'll admit we were also thinking of money. We chose the pub atmosphere and downtown location with that in mind, and it's paid off. And our menu doesn't have much home cooking on it— mostly sandwiches and a few soups—but I'm fond of food in general, I suppose. I like making it, and I like eating it."

He laughed, thinking her adorably cute. And he noticed that even though she wasn't a pound overweight, she also wasn't sporting that skinny-as-a-stick look some girls seemed to find so attractive. "I like a woman who eats," he confided in her. "A lot of the girls I've dated are the types who order a salad, no dressing, then watch me eat a huge steak. It makes for a pretty boring meal. I like to eat *with* someone."

She grinned. "I know what you mean. I don't mind eating alone, but if I'm sharing a meal with somebody, I want to really *share* the meal."

He nodded his agreement, surprised she actually understood what he was talking about, since he'd never really thought about it before right now.

"So what brings you to Cincinnati from a bustling place like Chicago?"

He kept it simple. "Just in the mood for a new start." It was one thing to confide your eating quirks to someone, but another entirely to admit a history of job failures, especially considering the circumstances of their own relationship so far. "Martin made me a good offer and I liked what I saw in the company."

She nodded—and surely he'd only imagined the disconcerted look on her face at the mention of Martin's name. "He's a good boss, and a good businessman. You'll be very happy there."

"By the way," Ryan said, "can I ask you something?" Part of him knew he shouldn't keep taking them back to that night, yet they were getting along so well that he didn't think it was unreasonable to seek clarification on this.

She looked a little worried, but said, "Okay."

"About you and Martin. Did you, uh, tell me you were engaged? I...missed some of the details when we were discussing it."

In reply, she pushed back a lock of stray hair, dropped her gaze, and said, "No, we're not engaged, at least not yet. He's proposed, but I haven't given him an answer."

He nodded. "I see." He'd thought that was what she'd said, but hadn't been sure, and he'd wanted to know how deeply he'd encroached. He still wasn't sure. And he wondered what was holding up her answer.

"And speaking of Martin, that reminds me…" She lifted one finger to her bottom lip, "He once showed me a program for another restaurant that had this nifty feature where you click on the item someone orders and all the little doo-hickeys pop up beside it, so no matter what someone wants or doesn't want, the server doesn't have to let anyone know anything special because it's all right there in the doo-hickeys." Then her pretty laughter washed over him. "Do you have any idea at all what I'm talking about?"

Swallowing the bite of baked potato in his mouth, he grinned. "Believe it or not, I do. It's a pop-up option box displaying a list of all the possible choices. Or doo-hickeys." He tossed a wink her way at that. *But stop it. No winking. Winking is totally off limits here. Get back to work.* "There are several ways it can be displayed, and I've got some templates for it loaded on the laptop, so I can let you take a look at them before I leave."

"Great," she said, and they shared another smile.

Unfortunately, though, Ryan had the scary feeling that maybe these were getting to be more than just normal, professional smiles. Especially this one, because their gazes locked. For too long. He felt it in his gut, and he couldn't help noticing how deep the blue of her eyes shone in the dim lighting of the kitchen as the sun started dipping toward the trees outside.

"Well…" she said, suddenly sounding nervous again.

"Dinner was great," he took over for her. "Thanks a lot. But I'd better show you those templates, then get out of your way for the evening."

He rose to his feet as she nodded in agreement, then wasted no time making his way back to the living room, to his laptop. Taking a seat, he pulled up the windows he wanted to show her. And as she dropped into the chair next to him, he threw himself back into professional mode, keeping his eyes on the computer. "This screen shows the most common way to display the options," he said, then clicked to open another window, adding, "and this layout takes up less space, but it's a little harder to see. There's a third method I personally like—" He reached to click the built-in mouse again—but suddenly Penny's small hand came down soft on his.

And his stomach clenched.

He swallowed and looked at her.

"Can you go back to the first option?" she asked. Then quickly drew back her hand as if realizing her error.

"Uh, yeah." His heart thumped like a seventh-grader's after being touched by a pretty girl. Eyes on the computer, he re-opened the first window. "Sorry if I was going too fast."

"No, no—I just wanted to compare the two I've seen so far. Can this print be made smaller?" She reached across him to point at the screen with one long, tapered finger, leaning closer than she had any time throughout the day.

"Not really." His senses began to swim with the lingering remnants of her perfume. "Makes it too hard for the computer to distinguish which option is being selected using touchscreen," he continued, but he thought his voice sounded sort of strangled now.

"Ah," she said. And although she started to pull her arm back, she did it way too slowly…slow enough to give him time to wonder, to consider—slow enough for him to make the impulsive decision to reach up and gently catch her wrist in his hand.

Angling his body toward hers made it even clearer how close to each other they were, how near her sweet eyes were, and her soft lips, parted now in something that was either passion or horror—he couldn't discern which. Time moved perilously slow. "I…" What? He what? "Oh hell," he murmured, then leaned forward to brush a short but tantalizing kiss across her lips.

Penny nearly melted as the feather-soft kiss swept through her. She hadn't expected it, but it had felt like a taste of heaven.

Except for one thing. It was wrong. Wrong, wrong, wrong.

Yanking her arm away, she kicked her feet out to send her desk chair rolling back from him and across the room. *"What do you think you're doing?"*

"Kissing you?"

She couldn't believe he'd done it, no matter how nice it might've felt. "You can't be kissing me!"

He nodded emphatically. "I know that, believe me."

"Then why did you do it?"

He gave a helpless sigh. "I have no idea."

The words left her even more stunned, only in a different way now, and she gasped, affronted, almost insulted. He was kissing her and he didn't even know why?

"What I mean is…"

"Yeah?"

His demeanor shifted. "I have a lot to lose here, you know. Like my job."

"Then don't you think kissing me is kind of a bad idea?"

"Absolutely." He suddenly looked determined, stalwart. "In fact, you're exactly the *last* kind of woman I need in my life."

She pulled in her breath sharply. "What's that supposed to mean?"

"Well," he began, lifting his gaze to hers, "frankly, you're too wild for me."

Her mouth dropped open. What had just happened here? And how could he think…? Well, okay, she supposed he actually had *every* reason to think she was wild, but she'd hoped she'd succeeded in explaining all that away the other night in the limo. Apparently not. "Listen, I told you that was just a one-time thing, a person I made up—"

"Sure, that's what you *told* me, but…"

She blinked in disbelief. "Are you calling me a liar?"

"I'm just saying…maybe you're a little wilder than you *think* you are."

"How would you know *what* I am?"

"Because you can't pretend the kind of stuff we did together."

His answer hit her low and hard, and she struggled for a reply, feeling defensive now that his words hung in the air. "Well, you were just as wild back, and—and you didn't even think I was someone you knew! At least I *thought* I knew *you*."

"Well, *I'm* not the one denying I'm wild. I'll admit I have the capacity to be wild, but I can't be that way anymore because I came to Cincinnati to settle down and be a good boy."

"If you're such a good boy, then why did you respond in the limo?" Aha—she had him now.

But when their gazes met, she quit feeling defensive. His eyes were such a warm, alluring shade of brown and he looked…sad. Desperate. *Passionate.*

"I couldn't resist," he finally admitted.

At least five feet stretched between them now. The fronds of a potted palm jutted in front of her face. There seemed safety in distance, but the expression in his eyes was enough to melt her and she suddenly wished the limo hadn't been dark, suddenly wished she'd had the pleasure of gazing into those eyes as heatedly as he gazed at her in this moment.

"Can't now, either," he said, getting to his feet. He closed the distance between them before Penny could even think, let alone protest. He reached for her hand, pulled her up to her feet next to him, then lifted his palms to her face.

Don't. The word echoed inside her, but didn't make it to her lips. An automatic response, but not what she really wanted.

The kiss was as gentle and fleeting as the one just a moment ago, but this time she savored it and let the pleasure trickle warmly through her body. "Oh…" she breathed. "This isn't me."

"Yes it is," he assured her—and she had no choice but to believe him when his next kiss came stronger, laced with the same thick desire she'd felt from him in the limo. She remembered the power, the restraint she'd felt in his kisses because she felt it now, too. And as she let herself get lost in the sensation of his mouth on hers, she longed to ask him to let go of that restraint and do *everything* to her.

"Your hair," he murmured in her ear as he sprinkled hot kisses just below. "It feels different than the other night."

She could barely find her voice. "I, uh, curled it then."

"It feels so silky. And it smells so good. I thought it was your perfume, but it's your hair."

"Sh-shampoo," she managed, yet his breathy hot voice had turned her knees to jelly and she didn't want to talk anymore. Lifting one hand to his cheek, she led his mouth back to hers, since even as much as she loved being kissed other places, at the moment she needed to feel his magnificent kiss on her lips.

She'd never imagined such powerful chemistry could

exist between two people, but it had the other night, even in the dark, and it pummeled her again now, making her feel completely won, completely weakened, completely at his mercy.

That was when he pulled back, breaking away from her.

"Oh God," he said, his gaze planted behind her as things came to a grinding halt. "I'm sorry."

Turning to look, she followed his eyes to the desk—to the large vinyl portfolio Martin had given her to store her paperwork on the system design. The words Schuster Software Systems were emblazoned across it in bold lettering.

"It's okay," she said, trying to come to grips with all of this—his fabulous kisses, and the fact that, for both of their sakes, she should *not* have been accepting them.

"No, it's not." He shook his head. "I can't do this."

"Neither can I, so we're even."

"I shouldn't have. I don't mean to be a jerk."

She spoke quietly, gazing again into eyes she thought more captivating each time she looked at them. "I don't think you're a jerk. I think we're just…in a weird situation." She paused, trying to clear her head. "We shouldn't be working together alone like this."

"I know, but how would we explain that to Martin?"

She glanced down. "That's the only reason I agreed to it—I couldn't figure out a way not to without looking suspicious." Raising her eyes back to him, she sighed. "But I think you should probably, uh, go now."

"Definitely."

Penny watched from the same spot where she'd just stood kissing him as he moved to the desk and hurriedly packed his laptop and all the notes he'd taken. Cramming it all in a leather bag, he strode to the front door, and only then did he stop to peer back at her.

"Penny," he said, looking desperate now, "I'm really sorry about kissing you. It was way out of line, weird situation or not. I just…" He sighed. "Well, never mind."

I'm just so freaking attracted to you I couldn't stop myself. But no good could come from that much honesty. He couldn't believe what he'd done, how much more difficult he'd just made things for both of them. What had he been thinking? But maybe that was the whole problem—he *hadn't* been thinking, he'd been *reacting*. To her. To everything about her. Damn his impulses.

"I'll see you tomorrow," he went on. "I mean, if you still want to work with me on this project. Because if you don't, I'll figure out some other way, some reason I can't do it."

She shook her head. "No, I…actually think we work well together…when we're not kissing." A nervous look came over her at that part, though.

So he tried to be reassuring. "So do I." It was the truth. "Goodnight," he said a little more brusquely than he'd intended as he headed out the door and proceeded down the front walk toward the curb, where he'd parked.

Pausing on the sidewalk, though, he looked over his shoulder to find her peering at him from just inside the front screen door. "One last thing," he said, feeling bolder than he had a right to.

"What's that?"

"Are you gonna marry him?" It was presumptuous as hell, but he had to know.

Behind the screen, she hesitated, and he felt his heart balancing precariously on her answer.

"No," she finally admitted in little more than a whisper. "Of course not. How could I now?"

A flood of relief washed through him. "Good," he said. Then he turned to walk on, taking a full two steps before he stopped and looked back again. "But that still doesn't change things between us. Because Martin's still my boss and you're still too wild for me." He'd just wanted to make sure they both knew where they stood.

"Hey, you're the one who keeps kissing me. All you have to do is stop."

"Right." He nodded. "And I will."

Still, even as he slid behind the wheel of his car, started the engine, and drove down the street, even as he reminded himself what was smart and right and rational, he couldn't help feeling inexplicably happy that she was no longer tied to some other guy.

Chapter Four

THE GREEN AWNINGS BEYOND THE PLATE GLASS WINDOWS shaded the sidewalk from the scorching mid-day sun. The lunch rush had ended not long ago and Penny heard the sounds of dishes being washed in the pub's kitchen.

She wiped down the bar, then glanced at the clock. Ryan was probably upstairs finishing his sandwich right now, probably still working in Martin's corner office, too. Thankfully, Grace had been at her desk when Penny had dropped off the lunches today, which kept her from having to lurk around the place. But whether or not she bumped into Ryan at Schuster Systems didn't really matter since he would be showing up at her house again in about an hour. She drew in a deep breath, then let it slowly back out, wishing she didn't feel so twitchy inside just thinking about him and all that had happened.

She kept reliving the moment when he'd brushed that impossibly soft kiss across her lips last night. It had melted through her like the thrilling purity of a *first* kiss, like first love, like she was sixteen and untouched and waiting for that first magical taste of romance. Every time she thought about it, she felt his mouth grazing hers again. But it would probably be wise to *stop* thinking about it because… Oh, poor Martin!

She hadn't known the truth about Martin until the words had left her yesterday. She wouldn't marry him. Couldn't marry him. Never even should have *considered* marrying him. She guessed being proposed to by a successful businessman, who was truly a nice person on top of it, had been flattering, and it had at least seemed worthy of some thought. But now any delusions of compatibility she'd been suffering had come to an end and she knew—

The rattle of a cup cut into her thoughts. "*Miss?*"

She looked up to find their last remaining lunch customer, a middle-aged businessman with messy hair and a wrinkled suit, waving his coffee cup at her from the end of the bar.

"Yes?"

"I *said* can I get a refill down here?" His dark eyebrows knit and his expression reminded Penny of an angry bear.

She was stunned to see she'd let his cup go empty and had apparently been ignoring him altogether. She *always* put customers first. Well, except for now, darn it. "Of course. I'm sorry." As she scurried toward him with the coffeepot, she could feel Patti's scowl from where her sister sat at a nearby table rolling silverware into napkins.

Great, now the whole Ryan/Martin fiasco was distracting Penny from *her* job, too. Still, thank goodness she'd figured out the right answer to Martin's proposal before it was too late.

So it's actually good this whole thing happened. She tried to convince herself while returning the coffeepot to its place. Wanting another guy so much had made the decision about marrying Martin clearer than anything else could have. *But now it's over because of Ryan's job.* Which was also good, because even after she officially broke things off with Martin, it would look awfully suspicious if she and Ryan were suddenly together, wouldn't it? And besides, Ryan had the ridiculous idea that she was too wild for him anyway. "Ha!"

"What?" Patti looked up, clearly perplexed, and Penny felt the rumpled businessman's questioning gaze, as well.

"Nothing." She shook her head lightly. She'd not exactly meant to cackle out loud, but when she thought about Ryan's accusation, it made her a little crazy inside.

After all, she'd been accused of a lot of things in her day. In elementary school, she'd been called Goody Two Shoes; in junior high, she'd been the Teacher's Pet; and in high school, she'd not dated a lot due to her reputation as a Nice Girl. Her family and friends had always labeled her with words like *dependable* and *hardworking*, and Patti always distinguished between the two of them by calling her The Sweet One. But no one had ever, by any stretch of the imagination, called Penny Halloran *wild*.

On the other hand, though, you did seduce the man in a limousine. The same man with whom she now had to design a computer system. The same man she couldn't kiss anymore—or have sex with anymore, either. She shook her head in disbelief, then tossed down her rag. The whole thing still didn't quite seem real, and her confusion over it had escalated with Ryan's kisses last night.

Finishing up a few last tasks behind the bar, Penny took a look around. After asking one of the waitresses, Lisa, to refill ketchup bottles when she got a chance, she said to Patti, "I've gotta run. Ryan will be over soon."

"Oh yeah. Time for your big computer date."

Penny blinked and hoped she looked normal. "What are you talking about?" It didn't help that Lisa and Bear-face down at the end of the bar were both listening, too.

"I'm not actually sure," Patti said, sounding irritatingly sleuth-like, "but I'm telling you, you get wide-eyed and sort of…*aloof* whenever that guy comes up."

Great, so she *didn't* look normal. "Do not," she protested. And she was arguing like a seven-year-old on top of it.

"Whatever you say," Patti replied in a sing-song voice that clearly said she wasn't buying it. And she almost got the idea that Patti thought Ryan was a better choice for her than Martin even without knowing him.

If only she could keep Martin on her mind for half as long as she thought about Ryan, maybe she wouldn't feel like such a rotten person. She dreaded turning down Martin's proposal, but once she did—and once she got through this system design with Ryan—well, then this would all be over.

And as for the little stab of pain in her chest when she thought of things with Ryan being over…that was probably just because Penny had never been particularly skilled at the art of casual dating. So it probably stood to reason that having *sex* with someone would cause at least a few odd, jarring feelings of infatuation. She *guessed* that was what you'd call it anyway, and she was a tad disconcerted that it seemed to be getting steadily worse.

But a little—or even a lot—of infatuation didn't matter. It *couldn't* matter. Ryan had made it clear that whatever attraction he felt for her wasn't enough to make him throw away his new job, and she couldn't blame the guy. After all, they barely knew each other.

A glance toward the bear-faced man found him looking amused by her discussion with Patti. "She's completely mistaken," Penny insisted. Then, mumbling a quick goodbye to Patti, she snatched up her purse and exited the restaurant before her sister could get any wiser that there was more to this story than met the eye.

———

RYAN TOOK a deep breath as he approached Penny's front door. It felt dangerous, like returning to the scene of a crime. He still couldn't believe he'd made such a lunkhead move yesterday. No wonder he kept losing jobs—he kept letting his wants get in the way of his responsibilities. What would it take before he learned his lesson? Another job loss? Another relocation? Maybe he'd *never* get it figured out and go broke in the process.

And as for whatever insane sense of relief he'd felt driving away from her house last night, he'd decided it was only because her decision had eased his guilt a little, made him feel a bit less like a trespasser. Because he'd meant what he'd said—she was too wild for him. And he couldn't keep screwing up every job he got, every chance someone gave him to build a career. So that meant...

You cannot think about her black bra. You cannot think about her slender curves. You can't even think about how soft her lips were yesterday or the intoxicating scent of her hair.

"Hi," Penny said, opening the door just as he was about to knock. "How are you?" Her eyes sparkled with a surprisingly friendly welcome and her lips looked ridiculously silken and inviting, which made them difficult not to think about. And, damn it, her hair still smelled that way. What was it—some kind of flower or fruit? He almost asked on impulse, when he jolted himself to a halt.

"I think it would be smart," he said on an exhale, "for us to skip the small talk and get right to work."

She looked surprised, perhaps irritated, even as her warm blue eyes took on that ridiculously innocent quality he'd noticed before. Yet she caught her breath and said, "Whatever you think is best."

Heading for her desk, he took a seat and set up his laptop, staying focused on the hardware in front of him.

"Something to drink?" she asked. "Not that I mean to make small talk. But it's hot outside and I thought you might be parched."

He resisted the urge to glance up at her, instead watching his computer screen blink to life. Still, from his peripheral vision, he saw that she wore her usual khaki shorts and a white sleeveless blouse, and that her hair was knotted up on top of her head in some sort of clip. A glimpse down revealed bare feet, which struck him as adorably sexy, although he had no idea why and absolutely refused to think about it. "No thanks," he said.

Did she just roll her eyes at him? He couldn't tell for sure, since he wasn't looking directly at her, but he could've sworn… "Did you just roll your eyes at me?" He swung his gaze onto hers.

Big mistake. When their eyes met, he felt it in his gut.

"As a matter of fact"—she planted her fists on her hips —"I did."

His heartbeat rose to his throat, but he merely lifted his eyebrows in question.

"Look, I understand the need to keep this all about business, but don't you think you're being a little extreme?"

"Nope, just ready to get to work," he claimed, forcing a smile, one of those professional ones that had come a little easier yesterday. He motioned to the laptop. "I want to show you the screens I put together last night."

When she slid into the chair next to his, finally allowing them to get Day Two of the project underway, Ryan exhaled a sigh of relief, then pointed to the laptop with an ink pen. "Okay, you recall the home screen. Now, when you click on the Accounting box"—he demonstrated —"you'll be asked for a password."

Together, they set up a password to use during the test phase, and she chose "prettypenny," explaining with a wistful smile that her grandpa had called her that when she was a little girl. "He and my grandmother had a farm down in Kentucky, about an hour south of here. The land is covered with strip malls and fast food restaurants now, but back then, there was a silo, and acres of tall corn, and a tire swing that hung from the big apple tree in front of their house, just for Patti and me."

Ryan himself had grown up in a rural farming community, and though Penny's memories of such surroundings sounded warmer than his own, it reminded him of good times. "My brother Dan and I had a swing, too, a wooden one. My dad sat down in it one day after we'd outgrown it and broke right through it."

They shared a smile over Ryan's recollection, and he decided he certainly agreed with her grandfather's nickname for her, but how the hell had they gotten off track so quickly? He purposely wiped the grin from his face and returned his eyes to the computer, ready to move into the accounting program once and for all.

An incredible sense of relief washed over him as he finally fell into full work mode, soon showing her the accounting elements he'd designed for the pub after leaving last night. He supposed his comfort came from having done this hundreds of times; working with clients had become second nature to him and explanations for each screen display rolled off his tongue with ease. But he didn't really care why, he only cared that it'd happened, that she hadn't distracted him with any more personal stuff, and that his professional side had taken back over before anything could go awry.

Every now and then, Penny uttered an "mmm-hmm" or an "ah" or asked a question, and Ryan made sure she understood the relevant features of each component before going to the next. Periodically, he asked her to give suggestions or point out things she disliked, taking notes and responding with suggestions of his own. By the time they'd walked through the screens he'd created, he felt a familiar sense of pride and satisfaction in his work.

"All right then," he said, "we've got the payables and receivables programs roughed in, let's move on to payroll. Like yesterday, I'll want to look at your notes, hear your thoughts, and we'll discuss ideas and look at some templates."

Glancing up, he saw her smile. "Dare I suggest a bathroom break?"

Ryan leaned back in his chair with a sigh and slowly let a conceding grin spread across his face. "I guess that's not a *totally* unreasonable request."

"And I, for one, am thirsty. Sure I can't tempt you?" She raised her eyebrows.

Okay, maybe he *had* been a little rigid earlier—it was easier to see in retrospect. But now they'd proven this could still be done, they could still work together like two normal human beings, two mature adults, even after yesterday's kisses. "All right. I'll have something cold."

As she got to her feet and padded from the room, he had to admit, things truly seemed *ordinary* here. Like yesterday, they were working together well, making good progress, and he was enjoying the interaction the same way he *usually* enjoyed client interaction. He might catch the occasional whiff of her hair now and then—what *was* that fragrance?—and he might notice the cute lilt in her voice when she caught on to how something worked, but overall, they'd fallen back into the roles of client and system designer with startling ease.

"I made some lemonade before you got here," her voice echoed from the kitchen.

"Sounds great." Peering at her hard drive resting upright on the floor beneath the desk, Ryan shrugged free of his suit jacket and got down on his knees. He started fiddling with the CD drive where, sure enough, one was lodged inside. It surprised him Martin couldn't have spent a little time making Penny's computer functional, but tomorrow, he'd bring a toolkit and take a closer look.

"It's from my grandma's secret recipe," she called, still in the other room.

"Your grandma has a secret recipe for lemonade?" he yelled back. "How can there be a secret to that?"

He continued to poke and prod at the CD as she replied. "If I told you, it wouldn't be a secret, would it?"

Her playful tone made him smile. "Is this the same grandma who lived in Kentucky?"

"Yep, same one."

"So you said the farm isn't a farm anymore. Did *all* the Hallorans get into the food and drink business?"

"No, just Patti and me. My father owns a hardware store, one of the last family-run ones in the city. And my grandparents are retired. But they probably *should* all be in the restaurant business. My grandmother and mom are wonderful cooks who taught me everything I know."

"What about Patti?" he asked over his shoulder. "They didn't teach *her*?"

Penny's short laugh resonated through the house. "Well, they tried, but it didn't work out. She handles more the management end of the business, the hiring, the firing, the banking. And I handle the menu and payroll...and now, I guess, the computer."

The glasses nearly slipped from Penny's hands when she entered the room to see Ryan down on all fours, his suit-clad butt in the air. She'd never really seen his butt before, but it looked nice. *Really* nice. Pinpricks of sensation skittered up her inner thighs. Right when things were going so smoothly, too, darn it.

After standing frozen in place for a moment, she lowered the two lemonades quietly to the corner of the desk, then headed for the bathroom. That's what she'd originally gotten up for, wasn't it? And she certainly didn't want to get caught gaping, or risk messing up what had, so far, been a nice, normal workday between them, despite what she'd felt upon his arrival. Familiar tendrils of desire had curled through her when she'd found him standing on her doorstep looking totally GQ, but she'd pushed them down, helped along by his brusque candor and his refusal to look at her. Now, however, the tension had eased—other than these sexy little pinpricks he never had to know about—and she hoped they could keep things on an even keel.

When she returned, he had, thankfully, risen back to his chair to take a sip of lemonade. "This is good."

But their eyes met, and something warm melted through her. Uh oh.

"Real lemons, ice not water, and lots of extra sugar," she unthinkingly blurted out, then hurried to take her seat beside him. Somehow it was easier then, when they were in the chairs, looking at the computers and not each other.

"Huh?" he asked.

She lifted her gaze, then lowered it just as quickly. "That's the recipe. In case you wanted to know."

Maybe he'd been right when he'd arrived. Maybe anything else *was* inviting trouble. Reaching across him for her own lemonade—dear God, she'd nearly brushed her breast against his arm—she took a long swallow and tried to let it cool her down inside.

She felt his glance from the corner of her eye. "I thought it was a secret."

Penny sighed. "Well, you seem trustworthy," she said, for lack of any better response.

When he reached to type something onto his laptop and accidentally bumped her arm, they both flinched uncomfortably, then exchanged lightning-quick looks.

"So…" he said.

"So…" she replied. Her heart beat too fast. Darn it, why couldn't they act normal around each other for longer periods of time?

"Let's talk payroll," he suggested hurriedly.

"Yes, let's."

———

WHEN RYAN LOOKED past her toward the window, Penny raised her gaze as well.

"It's getting dark," he said.

It startled her to see dusk falling outside; the lights she'd turned on this afternoon had kept them from noticing the gradual change. She glanced to the mantle clock. "I can't believe it's so late. Almost nine."

He gave his head a regretful shake. "My fault. I get a on a roll, and I totally lose track of time."

"No need to apologize," she assured him. "I'm just surprised. I had no idea we'd worked that long." Although when she thought about it, they'd covered a lot. They'd gone over her manual payroll procedures and discussed how to best represent them in the system, then they'd moved on to her notes about budget and the monthly balance sheets. Even as the comfort level had grown steadily deeper, though, she'd remained aware of her attraction to him.

Now his smile trickled through her like a hot drink. "It's always a good sign when time flies, you know. Every now and then, I get into a situation where it's just the opposite, where one hour with a client feels like five, and that always means we're getting nothing accomplished. But I feel really positive about our work here, and I think we'll create a system you'll like."

So…it would seem he really *had* relaxed now. He could smile at her without acting antsy or uncomfortable. Which meant she was the only one here still feeling…things. Tingly, ripply, urge-like things.

But that's good. Heartbreaking in a way, since it was always nice to think a guy wanted you, but hadn't she decided for Ryan's sake, and for Martin's sake, that Ryan was right and nothing more could happen between them? She made herself smile back, glad—in theory anyway— that things felt more normal again, like when they were both buried in the work.

Although…did she just sense some slight, barely perceptible change in the air?

No, probably not. It was likely just wishful thinking on her body's part. The little thrill that had zipped down through her when they'd shifted their gazes from the computer to one another just now probably meant nothing. The fact that his eyes, squarely planted on hers, seemed to be filling with something like…*heat* was probably entirely in her imagination.

"Can I offer you dinner?" She regretted the invitation even as it left her, but it'd just tumbled out. She rushed ahead, anxious to fill the suddenly awkward moment with more words. "Usually, I would've eaten hours ago. If you don't mind more pot roast, I could make some sandwiches with it. Or if you're ready to take off, that's fine, too. Whatever you want."

She actually thought he looked tempted—until he said, "Thanks, but I should definitely get going."

Penny simply nodded. *Definitely*. The conviction in his voice brought her back down to earth, and considering what had happened last night after eating together, she couldn't argue with his unspoken logic.

He drew his eyes away as he shut his laptop. "Can I ask you something before I go, though?"

"Okay."

"I was wondering…how you're doing over the Martin thing. Your decision not to marry him, I mean."

"Oh." The question caught her off-guard, though she hardly knew why since Martin's proposal had been the entire basis of their bizarre relationship so far. "I'm doing fine."

So fine, in fact, that I keep wanting you—in a big way. She didn't know if it was the dusky lighting and the falling of night or if it was simply the culmination of urges she'd been battling all day, but as her desires escalated, it seemed like a good time to put some distance between them.

She left the desk and moved casually to her overstuffed couch. That way she couldn't do something crazy like touch him if the unstoppable urge arose. Especially now that he seemed so in control, so totally uninterested in her physically. Nothing would be worse than making a move and getting shot down.

"When are you going to tell him?" Ryan asked, slipping the laptop in its case.

"Whenever he calls from Vegas." And, actually, she was surprised she hadn't heard from Martin yet—it was Tuesday and he'd left on Friday. She'd expected a call over the weekend, but at least the delay had given her time to work on what she was going to say.

"Isn't that kind of cold?" Ryan asked, turning his chair to face her. It didn't sound like an accusation exactly, just an honest question.

She took a deep breath before replying. "Maybe, but this way, he won't have to break down in front of me, you know? And I'd rather get it over with, not put it off."

His gaze focused directly on her now, unnervingly so. "I'm sorry, Penny, if I ruined something good between the two of you."

And her stomach dropped. It had never even occurred to her that Ryan didn't know the very brief history she shared with Martin, or how unexpected his proposal had been. Besides not wanting Ryan to feel badly, it also seemed important to let him know what they'd done together wasn't nearly so awful as if she'd been in a real, viable, long-term relationship. "You didn't." She shook her head emphatically. "We'd only been dating a few months."

He shrugged. "It doesn't always take months to have a serious relationship. It happens all the time. People meet and fall in love like *that*." He snapped his fingers.

It made her wonder, for the first time, about Ryan's love life. "Has that ever happened to you?"

"Me? No." He shook his head almost as if the idea were preposterous, even though he'd brought it up himself. "I *know* people who it's happened to, but I'm not sure I could ever fall in love that quickly myself."

"Why?" Suddenly she was perplexed, and somewhere deep inside, a little hurt. Maybe she'd hoped this sensual energy between them was about more than sex, that he was harboring some secret, budding affection for her that he just hadn't had the courage to mention.

He raised his gaze, as if confiding in her. "I guess maybe I'm just cautious."

Did that mean he'd been hurt before? "Bad relationships in the past?" she ventured.

He shook his head. "Nothing like that." He smiled slightly, his expression turning mischievous. "Maybe cautious is the wrong word. Maybe it's more like…reluctant. There's nothing too heavy in my past, and I guess I like it that way. I like keeping things light and being on my own at the end of the day, if you know what I mean."

Yes, she knew exactly what he meant. He wasn't looking for a relationship. He'd told her he'd come here to be a good boy, that he didn't want anything wild in his life, so apparently women were on the back burner for him completely right now. Or he wanted them to be anyway. Because there was, of course, her, and what had happened, and what, she supposed uncertainly, could still happen…

Oh, darn it, that proved it; she totally still wanted him. Desire hummed through her veins even as she sat talking with him. "Well, despite what you may think, things were very casual between me and Martin. And the truth is, I didn't know him all that well, romantically speaking."

Ryan tilted his head. "But in the limo…"

"Yeah?"

"Well, you didn't seem shy."

She tried to swallow her embarrassment, but failed. And considering how much personal stuff Ryan knew about her already, she saw no reason not to explain this, as well. "As I started to tell you then, I wanted to find out…if Martin had a wild side, too."

When she least expected it, a slow, almost wicked smile unfurled across Ryan's face.

"What?" she asked in bewildered response.

"So you admit it. You *are* wild."

Oh boy. She released a long, exasperated sigh. "I admitted I had a wild *side*. That's different than being wild."

"You said you were living out a fantasy," he reminded her.

"So? Everyone has fantasies."

"But"—he raised one finger in the air—"not everyone lives them out."

Penny drew in her breath, wishing she could break her gaze with his, wishing she wanted to. Yet his unexpected words were settling deep inside her, easing their way into cracks and crevices she'd never peered into before.

Oh God, it was true. She'd read enough articles in Cosmo and Glamour to know most people—women anyway—never really attempted to live out their fantasies. She suspected most women kept them inside and saw them as impossibilities, even as things they didn't truly want to happen. But the moment she had started exploring *hers*, she'd known they were things she really wanted, experiences she truly desired, adventures she intended to have. And her own thoughts a moment ago only seemed to confirm it; she'd been sitting there wanting Ryan even though she knew that *he* couldn't, and *she* couldn't, and that it was all wrong.

Suddenly feeling as transparent as a negligee, she thrust herself up from the couch and walked across the room toward the foyer, anxious to escape his gaze. She had no reply to what he'd just said, but it was as if he'd just shone a flashlight into the darkest corner of her soul. Coming to a stop before the mirror near the door, she fumbled for something to do with her hands, some way to distract herself from the nervous tension swirling through her. She adjusted the leaves of a philodendron spilling from a pot on a shelf next to the mirror, then reached below, idly turning on the radio on her old retro stereo.

The low sounds of Marvin Gaye singing "Let's Get It On" wafted through the room.

Penny bit her lip. This probably wasn't a good moment for the sexiest song of all time, yet for some reason, she couldn't bring herself to change it.

That meant nothing, though. It didn't mean she was wild, nor did it mean she was waiting for something to happen here. She just didn't want to look panicky, that was all. She didn't want to do anything to let him know how tense and how…utterly sexual she suddenly felt.

And if she really *were* wild, wouldn't she start doing something like swaying her hips back and forth to the music, or stripping to it or something? As it was, she clamped both fists to the edge of the mid-century console stereo and held on for dear life, lest she faint from nervousness. Hardly the act of a wanton woman.

"I know about the limo now"—Ryan's voice came from behind her, low…and sexy…and *close*—"but what other kinds of fantasies do you have, Penny?"

She lifted her gaze to the mirror to find him standing directly behind her. His eyes burned with everything she felt, that same desire, that same undeniable want. And one defensive part of her wished she could tell him he'd just crossed a line by asking her something so deeply personal —but considering what they'd done together in the limo, and that she'd told him it was a fantasy come true, she didn't really think he had. And she wished she were more offended by his forwardness, but she just wasn't…because nothing with Ryan ever felt wrong. Not from that first touch, that first kiss. It was a startling revelation. Everything with him always felt good and right and meant to be, no matter how much they both knew it shouldn't happen.

She should've been asking him what he thought he was doing, reminding him of his own rules, that they couldn't do this. Instead, though, she skipped ahead to something that came from deeper inside, something she needed to make clear to him once and for all—and then maybe they'd *both* understand it. "Take a good look at me, Ryan," she said, peering at him in the mirror. "I'm the girl next door. The teacher's pet. I'm June Cleaver and Mary Tyler Moore and all the Waltons rolled into one." She spread her arms helplessly. "I am *not* wild."

Never letting his eyes leave hers, Ryan reached up and pulled the clip from her hair, letting her tresses fall down her back in a rush. Then, placing his hands on her shoulders, he gently turned her to face him. Without pause, his fingers moved to the buttons on her blouse, where he undid one, then the next, then the next. She tried to make herself protest, step away from him, anything—but her skin tingled with too much pleasure. *I am not wild, I am not wild, I am not wild.* A silent mantra. Yet her body didn't seem to know that at the moment.

"Maybe you're not wild on the outside," he said, his voice husky. "But underneath…"

As Ryan freed the last button on her blouse, he pushed it open to reveal a lacy lavender bra. The sight stole his breath and proved his point better than any words he could've spoken. Who'd have thought Penny the Sandwich Girl would wear *this* under her simple shirts?

Then he remembered the other night, the sexy lace beneath his fingertips. And when he put that whole experience together with this discovery, he knew without doubt that everything he'd said about her was true—she was wild at heart. It went deeper than one night, deeper than one fantasy—and maybe *she* didn't know it, but he did. Nothing he'd ever done had felt sexier than pushing the blouse from her shoulders, unveiling the sensual woman beneath the façade of simplicity.

Tracing one fingertip down the lavender strap of her bra, he followed the seam over the rounded ridge of her breast to the center where a tiny lavender bow connected the cups. "You're so bad for me," he whispered.

Her voice trembled. "I see it the other way around."

Part of him wanted to argue, to remind her that her commitment to Martin was over and she no longer had anything to lose, whereas he still had everything at stake. He wanted to tell her just how *good* for her he could be, how he could *prove* to her how wild she was, if only his job didn't stand in the way. But he feared any further words would bring this to a screeching halt.

And even though he knew he was committing career suicide, at the moment he was like an addict who couldn't see reason, who only wanted one more taste of her, one more touch. The more time he'd spent with her today, the more they'd talked—be it about work or families or the little asides she'd shared from time to time about her neighborhood or the hot weather or needing to water her flowers—the more something had begun to build inside him. He liked her. He liked her laughter. He liked the innocence that draped so honestly over her more sensuous side. He liked that she was smart and talented, which showed in the way she ran her business, yet equally genuine and down-to-earth, making the same lemonade as her grandmother. And he also liked her wild side, which had caused something else to gather in him without his quite knowing it, too—a compulsion, a driving need, to free her hidden passion beneath his hands.

Lowering them to her slender waist, he deftly unbuttoned her shorts, then lowered the zipper. He watched his fingers working, but heard her breathing above. He wanted to do this gradually, leisurely, wanted to rediscover that slow, intense heat they'd shared in the limo, everything else be damned.

Dropping to his knees at her side as the music urged him on, he reached up to ease the shorts over her hips. She gazed down, biting her lip in what he read as sweet, sexy surrender, and gently wriggled free of them. The motion turned his knees to mush, especially when he discovered the matching lavender thong she wore beneath, the lacy elastic disappearing down the center of her rounded bottom.

This woman didn't think she was wild? This woman didn't know how incredibly hot she was? It seemed impossible, but he felt bound and determined to show her, to make her know it, just like *he* did.

Leaning forward, he placed a feathery kiss on her bared hip and listened as she pulled in her breath above. And then he used his hands to turn her, turn her, until he found himself lowering another tender kiss, this one to her rear—and then another, and another. His chest tightened as his desire wound tighter and hotter. When she arched her backside toward him, he glanced up to see her arms raised overhead like some sensual statue, a work of erotic art. As he rained more soft kisses across her perfect bottom, her sexy sighs drowned out the music altogether until all he knew was her body, her sounds, her scent, the sensuality that almost dripped from her.

"You're so hot," he breathed.

"I...I don't do these things." she whispered from above. Just as he'd feared, he should've stayed quiet.

"It's okay, Penny," he said soothingly, nibbling around the thin strip of lavender at her hips. "If you're still afraid I'll judge you in some way, I won't—I swear. We're both human."

"It's not that. It's just that...I really *don't* do these things. Not without knowing a guy. And even then..." she moaned when he moved his kisses to the other side of her rear, "...it's not like this."

"What do you mean?"

"No man has ever...undressed me in my foyer and started kissing me this way."

He leaned forward to place a kiss at the small of her back that made her gasp, yearning to make her understand what was going on inside her, yearning to help her release it. "Then why are you doing these things with *me?*"

She gazed over her shoulder, down into his eyes. "I guess it *feels* like I know you," she admitted. "I don't know why."

"I feel the same way," he told her. It was true. From the beginning.

"But we...don't. Not really."

"We're starting to. And I want to know you better."

"Yet there's still Martin to think about and—"

"Shh," he said, desperate not to let anything more interfere with the raging attraction between them. He hooked his thumbs gently into the elastic at her waist, his voice a mere growl. "Don't let any of that matter. Don't let it stop this."

At that precise second, the phone rang, and they both flinched. "Damn it," he groused as the trilling noise sliced through his pleasure.

And she gasped. "Maybe it's Martin."

At this, he could only ground out a muttered curse.

Penny tripped free from the shorts at her ankles and took off toward the phone in the kitchen—as Ryan simply pushed to his feet, then shoved frustrated hands back through his hair.

"Hello?" Penny quaked as she thrust the receiver

beneath her ear. *Please don't let it be Martin.* She didn't think she could deal with that right now.

"Hey, what's up? You sound out of breath." It was Patti, thank God. But then, in a way, that was just as bad.

"I was just…" *About to have sex with a stranger for the second time in a week.* Oh dear, she really *had* been about to do that! Her! Good girl Penny Halloran! "I was just…cleaning. I was…up to my elbows in suds and I ran to get the phone."

"You were cleaning? At nine o'clock on a Tuesday night?"

Penny really didn't think it sounded so preposterous. Some people cleaned at odd hours. "Is there some rule against that?"

"No, but I just think it's weird."

"Well, I want to get back to it, so did you call for some purpose?"

"I just wanted to tell you I'll be late tomorrow. I have a dentist appointment I forgot about. But hey, far be it from me to interrupt a late night cleaning frenzy, so I won't keep you."

Penny felt bad for lying to Patti so much lately, not to mention that she probably seemed extremely suspicious. But considering that she stood in the kitchen in only her underwear and Ryan still waited for her in the foyer, she took the out. "Okay. See you tomorrow. Bye."

Hanging up, she drew a deep breath and glanced toward the doorway, girding herself for whatever would come next. She couldn't quite believe she was about to let this happen, and she didn't know where Penny the Sweet One had disappeared to, but she wanted this. Even with Patti's interruption, even with her fears that it had been Martin calling, her body still hummed with the passion it seemed only Ryan loosed in her. She'd broken away to answer the phone out of something like fear. The disruption had felt like one last chance to stop this. But now that she'd done it, taken the call, given it a chance to *be* stopped —she realized she truly didn't want that. Not anymore. And maybe she never really had in the first place.

She bit her lip as she rounded the corner, suddenly feeling as wild and sexy as Ryan kept telling her she was.

Chapter Five

THE INSTANT PENNY MET RYAN'S EYES, SHE KNEW everything had changed. He wore that guarded, regretful expression she'd seen on his face before as he held her blouse out to her. Painfully aware of the silence now filling the room—he'd turned the music off while she was away —she took it from him.

Lifting one hand to her cheek, he spoke low and deliberate. "I love the way you look right now, Penny. And I love how wild you are, even if you don't see it. But I have to go."

"Oh." She only hoped the hurt bubbling inside her didn't show.

"I like you so much—you don't *know* how much. But this is…"

"Wrong?" she supplied.

"Right," he said, meeting her eyes briefly before lowering his gaze. "I can't risk my job this way. I wish I could, but I can't."

"I understand," she replied, but her voice sounded hollow to her because she still wanted him to stay, still wanted things to be the way they were when they forgot about Martin and Schuster Systems. Suddenly feeling naked in her lavender undies, she thrust her arms into her shirt, then held it closed in front.

Ryan moved to the desk to retrieve his laptop and jacket, then turned to leave. He paused to lower a conciliatory kiss to her forehead as he passed by, but she hardly noticed, too stunned by how quickly things had shifted. A second later, the door shut behind him and she felt more alone than she had in a very long time.

She knew why he had to go; she knew it made sense. And earlier, she'd been all about trying to do the sensible thing, for the sake of his job—and for Martin's sake, too. But as she buttoned up her blouse, she still ached inside. As it turned out, there *was* something worse than making a move and getting shot down. Having *him* make a move, then change his mind.

He'd left her on the night after they'd had sex in the limousine, and that had been fine. In fact, it had been the only reasonable thing about the entire evening. And he'd left her again last night after the passionate kisses they'd shared, and she'd still understood why it had to be, and that had strengthened her.

But tonight, everything was different. Maybe because she'd spent more time with him now. Maybe because she'd confided her fantasies in him—more than confided, lived them. No other human beings knew those secrets and it had created a certain, unplanned intimacy between them. Maybe because throughout the day they had talked, shared things, and she'd started feeling more and more comfortable with him. And perhaps that meant her physical attraction toward him, even the irrational sense of infatuation, was beginning to be *more*.

Sinking into an easy chair, she buried her head in her

hands. An emotional attachment to this guy—a guy who worked for Martin—was the last thing she needed. And her stomach clenched to know that when forced to make a choice between her and the job, he chose the latter.

And yet, what did she expect? Who was she to him? Nobody but a girl who had thrown herself into his lap in a dark car, ripped his clothes off and attacked him. How had she gotten herself into this mess?

She steeled herself with a deep breath and pushed to her feet. She wasn't going to think about this anymore; she couldn't right now. She had something more important to do, something which suddenly couldn't wait any longer.

She didn't know Martin's conference schedule, but she knew she wanted to get her loose ends with him tied up this very minute. At least then she'd feel a little less guilty. Things were messy enough without his proposal still hanging over her head.

He was staying at the Bellagio—and she imagined him relaxing in his room at this hour, maybe ordering some room service, catching up with the day's news in a fluffy white hotel robe. She placed the call to him with vigor, ready to take action. As she waited for him to answer, she clumsily maneuvered back into her shorts, the phone pressed to one ear, deciding the conversation would be easier without reminders that she'd just had her clothes off with someone else.

Settling on the couch, she tensed when the ringing abruptly ended, then took a deep, preparatory breath... only to hear his voicemail message begin, "You've reached Martin Schuster of Schuster Systems. Please leave a message."

Martin, I'm sorry, but I just can't marry you. She opened her mouth to speak, then let out a huge sigh and hung up, every ounce of boldness evaporating. Telling him on the phone was one thing, but leaving it as a recording just wasn't human, no matter how desperate she was for closure.

"Oh, would you just call me, you idiot!"

Staring at the phone in her hand, Penny tried to get hold of herself. Her entire body still tingled with crazed mixtures of excitement and disappointment and anticipation and failure. She felt her eyes growing wet, but refused to cry—and when a tear rolled down her cheek, she obstinately wiped it away. Everything inside her felt crazy.

Eat, you need to eat. It was late and she was probably running on empty.

As she moved to the kitchen, still feeling defiant, she decided she'd had enough pot roast for one week. Given the unusual circumstances of the evening—and of her whole life lately—she was going to throw all dietary caution to the wind and indulge herself. Grabbing a tray from the pantry, she loaded it up with horrible, wonderful things. A plate of brownies. A tub of French vanilla ice cream. A dish of strawberries and an extra large bowl of Cool Whip.

Now, calm down. Be good to yourself. Try to enjoy this. Try to feel like you again. Normal Penny, who owned a business and behaved professionally at all times. Good Girl Penny, who didn't sleep with strangers. Pretty Penny, the Sweet One, the apple of her grandpa's eye. Yes, it would be good to get back on more familiar emotional ground.

Carrying the tray down the hall to her old-fashioned bathroom, she let the warm tones of room soothe her. After balancing her tray on the rounded edge of the big claw-footed tub, she went to the old pedestal sink and splashed cool water on her face, glad she'd conquered her tears.

Next, she started a bath, pouring a long stream of her

favorite bubble bath beneath the warm running water. After which pulled her hair up into a big clip, then scurried to the foyer to turn the radio back on. The same station from earlier still played slow soul, more Marvin, "Sexual Healing" this time. She didn't bother changing it, though, deciding to concentrate on the song's tranquil rhythm rather than the words.

When the tub was almost full, she turned off the water, slipped back out of her clothes, then stepped into the luxurious bubbles. Sinking into the suds, she leaned her head back and let the music sedate her. She occasionally reached for a strawberry or brownie, either dipping it in the softening ice cream or the smooth Cool Whip before putting it in her mouth.

This is nice. Decadent and relaxing all at once. *Who needs a hot guy or great chemistry or fabulous sex to have good time? Not this girl.*

Except…uh-oh.

As the sudsy water caressed her skin, the rich foods seemed to…somehow heighten her sensual awareness from the inside. The sensations hardly brought back Normal Penny—instead, darn it, they seemed to contour the newer, more daring version of herself she'd so recently uncovered.

But maybe that was okay, maybe not an uh-oh after all. Because it was still nice, albeit in a different way than she'd intended. And even though she knew each sensuous flutter inside her was probably just a leftover frustration from Ryan's departure a little while ago, she didn't care. She preferred to think of it as something she was feeling *by* herself, *for* herself.

After eating her fill of the sweets, she stretched out in the tub more completely, luxuriating more deeply in the moist bubbles, and let her mind begin to wander. Her thoughts drifted back to Ryan and the foyer—although she refused to think about the hurt that still lingered inside her, so instead she found herself envisioning the things that might have happened if the phone hadn't rung. She even imagined about placing a sexy call to Ryan, using her feminine wiles to somehow lure him back.

Then, other, wilder pictures entered her head, more fantasies, some she was already familiar with, others that were brand new—and somehow just the very act of thinking about them somehow made her feel...unfettered, free. Admittedly, none of this was doing much to lower her level of frustration, yet she still couldn't stop her mind from exploring all the stirring new possibilities that floated through her brain.

And then she gasped, bolting upright in the tub, the move sloshing water over the edge.

Was it possible? Could it be true?

All these fantasies, running rampant in her head...

The sexy undies she always wore, even though no one usually saw them...

And she'd seduced a man in a limousine—she'd done that, really made it happen.

And, oh, the positively *wicked* things she wanted to do to Ryan, if only he would let her.

A sharp tingle whisked through her body, traveling from the top of her head to the tips of her fingers and toes, and Penny knew without doubt it really *was* true. Everything inside her pointed to it, and she couldn't believe she'd been so blind for so long. She could only assume this was something that had been buried deep inside her for years, and it was finally fighting its way free.

She bit her lip at the stunning revelation that she didn't know herself as well as she thought...and that she really *wasn't* such a good girl after all.

RYAN STOOD PEERING into his refrigerator, wishing he saw something to eat. Instead, he found beer, soda, orange juice and butter. He'd stayed so busy at work that he hadn't even gotten unpacked yet, much less found time to make a serious trip to the grocery. Closing one door and opening another, he explored the freezer with a little more success. He'd grabbed a box of pizza rolls and some frozen garlic bread at a convenience store the other night when he'd stopped for drinks. Turning on the oven, he found a pizza pan and emptied the contents of both packages onto it. Not exactly pot roast, but all things considered, it would do.

While the food was in the oven, he shed his suit and tie, changing into a pair of old gym shorts and a T-shirt. Moving back through the spacious yet bare-looking condo that didn't quite feel like home yet, he realized he was actually more comfortable at Penny's house. He still hadn't unloaded most of his boxes, the cabinets were empty, as were the walls and tabletops, too—whereas at Penny's, everything was warm and tidy and inviting.

But then he shook his head. *Don't even go there.* He'd been smart to leave, smart to put his job and his future first.

Of course, being so smart had also left him feeling like a jerk, because he'd seen the pain in her eyes and he'd ignored it. Just walked away.

Grabbing a beer from the fridge, he popped the top and let out a sigh. He was an ass. For approaching her in the foyer like that, for letting his desires get the best of him, for running out on her like some kind of coward the moment he'd come to his senses.

It would've been so damn easy to stay, and he wished

he were in bed with her right now, holding her afterward, talking, laughing—he hadn't gotten to do any of that the first time. He loved Penny's laugh. And he loved the way she scrunched up her nose when something irritated her. Even her *feet* had been sexy. It was just a shame she hadn't turned out to be the simple girl he'd originally thought.

The way he'd wanted her tonight had nearly ripped him apart inside, and the unfulfilled ache still lingered between his legs. But just like *last* night, even as much as he regretted the reality of their situation, he'd known leaving was best. Even as that phone call had ruined something close to sheer perfection, it had also saved him.

Just then, he caught sight of the little red light blinking across the room. He was surprised to see he had a phone message, unsure who would be calling him. Unless it was Penny, and he doubted she even had his number. Or Martin, God forbid. He wasn't sure how he'd ever face his boss again, but at least he had a few more days before he had to. A few more days to try to get this whole thing with Penny into the past, where it wouldn't seem quite so overwhelming.

Taking a long swallow of beer, he crossed the ceramic tile and pressed the playback button. "Hello Ryan, it's your mother." She always did that, always told him who she was, as if he wouldn't recognize her voice. "Just calling to say hi and see if you're getting settled. Your father and I will talk to you soon."

According to the clock on the microwave, it was almost ten, so if he called back right now, he'd catch them before they went to bed. Not that he was particularly in the mood to chat with his parents. Oh, he loved them dearly and knew they loved him, too, but he had enough stuff bugging him already without hearing the latest wonderful news about his older brother, which any conversation with his mom and dad was sure to produce.

Thinking about that old swing in the yard today had briefly reminded him that once upon a time he and Dan had been close, but that was ancient history. Just like with his parents, he loved his brother, yet they'd grown apart. They were very different people and their lives had led them down opposite paths. Dan was the smart one, the selfless one, the settled one—the perfect son. He was everything two parents could hope for, and though Ryan knew his mom and dad didn't intend for him to feel Dan was their favorite, he still did.

Taking another swig of beer, Ryan let reinforce in his mind just how badly he didn't want to screw up again. He'd never been a bad kid, but it was hard living up to a brother like Dan; no matter what good things Ryan accomplished, it was the bad that seemed to stand out next to his brother's perfection. He could still hear the disappointment in his father's voice, along with his mother's despairing sigh, when he'd told them about losing his job at ComData. Not support, not encouragement, not speaking up in his defense—just disappointment. And the even worse part was that they hadn't sounded very surprised.

Grabbing up the phone before he talked himself out of it, he dialed the same phone number his family had had since he was a little boy.

"Hello?" His father's greeting sounded gruff and scratchy, reminding Ryan that they were getting older.

"Hey, Dad."

"Ryan," he said in recognition. "Here's your mother."

Good old Dad, never much for small talk.

"Ryan—hello," his mother said a few seconds later.

"Hi Mom. Sorry to call so late, but I just got in."

"That's all right—Dan and Carol just left. We had

some pie and then helped them pick out songs for church this Sunday. Did you know Dan is leading the choir now?"

Figures. "No. No, I didn't."

"Well, Miss Higgins has a bad hip and can't stand up that long anymore, so Dan volunteered to take over. And just in time, too, because the Summer Songfest is only two weeks away and the choir has to be ready."

Ryan found himself nodding into the phone even though he knew his mother couldn't see him. It was an old habit left over from when he'd lived at home, because he'd grown tired of saying, "Yeah," and "Uh-huh," when listening to constant praise of Dan the Man. His parents never seemed to notice his lack of response.

"Well," Ryan said, "but I just wanted to let you know things are going fine here. The job is great and I really like the company."

"Are you eating?"

Ryan laughed. "Not at the moment, Mom." Worry over his eating habits was the one way his mother showered concern on him. If he was at home, she plied him with food, and if he wasn't, she was lecturing him about it. "But don't worry, I've got something in the oven right now and I'm keeping myself adequately fed."

"Junk food, I'll bet."

He spent another fleeting thought on Penny's pot roast and said, "Not all the time. Don't worry, I'm fine. And hey"—time to change the subject—"the condo is great. You guys should think about making a trip down here in the fall."

His mother stayed quiet. Predictably. It had been the same every time he'd invited them to Chicago, too. Finally, she said, "We'll see." Which really meant "no." They only wanted to see him when he came home, when he was willing to revisit *their* life—as opposed to actually checking out *his* life, the one he'd gone out and built on his own. Sometimes he felt they only wanted a relationship with him when it was on their terms.

"Okay, Mom," he said. "I'm kinda tired, though, so I won't keep you."

They said their goodbyes and Ryan hung up feeling as hollow as such conversations usually left him. Oh well, at least the call was out of the way now.

Sniffing the air, Ryan caught a whiff of something hot…burning! Plunking his beer can on the counter, he rushed to the stove and yanked open the oven door.

Damn. Nothing like crunchy pizza rolls.

Fumbling for a potholder—thankful he'd even remembered to use one the way his night was going—he rescued the pan from the oven and decided the garlic bread didn't look like a total loss, just a little brown around the edges.

Rather than hunting for a plate, he just took the whole pan to the table, lowering it to a woven placemat, then grabbed his beer and sat down. He'd planned on doing some work on Penny's system tonight, but as he popped the first crisp pizza roll into his mouth, he decided he really *was* too tired; he was going to go to bed and get some rest.

And wake up with a new attitude. No more messing around, no more taking chances, no more wild women, no more *anything* that could screw up his life in any way.

He might resent his parents, but he still couldn't help wanting, *wishing*, to make them proud. And hell, maybe he wanted to make *himself* proud, too.

None of this was Penny's fault—okay, except maybe for that first incident in the limo—but either way, he had to be done with this, done with *her*. She might be cute and fun and sweet and sexy, but that didn't matter. Starting tomorrow, no more Penny. Well, no more Penny outside of their working relationship, something he didn't have much of a choice in. And to facilitate that, he was going to set a new number one priority—get Penny's computer fixed, so they wouldn't have to meet at her house any longer.

———

"YOU'VE REACHED Martin Schuster of Schuster Systems. Please leave a message."

Penny sneered in response to Martin's voice as she stood behind the closed door of the pub's office the next morning. But today she had enough wits about her to do as he instructed. "Martin, call me as soon as you get this." Then she disconnected and exited the office, where it appeared a small mid-morning rush on coffee and danishes was just dying down. It was raining outside—the only thing to cool the city in a week—and rain always brought in the coffee drinkers.

"Sorry," she said to Patti, who'd handled the whole thing alone right on the heels of her dentist appointment. None of the servers clocked in until eleven.

"No biggie," her sister replied, wiping her hands on a towel. Penny joined her behind the bar, and as the last customer exited, paper bag in hand, Patti lifted her gaze. "So what were you cleaning last night?"

Penny blinked, feeling as if her sister had just shone a bright light directly into her eyes. "Nice segue."

Patti snapped her fingers repeatedly. "Come on, come on, answer me, quick. What did you clean?"

"Uh…floors," Penny claimed, wishing she had more experience at lying.

"With a mop or on your hands and knees?"

Recalling having said she was up to her elbows in suds, she smugly replied, "Hands and knees."

Patti reached down to grab one of Penny's wrists and

they both looked down at five perfectly manicured nails. "Liar," Patti said.

Penny sighed. She truly hated being dishonest with her sister, but she still couldn't tell her about what had happened in the limo because the whole event continued to feel so intimate, so private, so painfully personal.

"Do I have to twist this," Patti asked, still gripping Penny's arm, "or are you gonna spill?"

Penny narrowed her eyes, took a deep breath, and decided to tell her sister…as much as she could. "You want to know what I was really doing when you called last night? Fine. I was standing in the foyer making out with Ryan in my underwear. Happy now?"

Patti's jaw dropped and Penny took perverse pleasure in having shocked her. "Ryan the sexy computer guy?"

"That's the one."

Patti sucked in her breath and tightened her grip on Penny's wrist. "Pen, does this mean you're not…"

"Marrying Martin? Correct. I'm not." She glanced at the clock above the bar. "Now I only wish he would call, so I could tell him."

"He doesn't know yet?" Patti blinked.

And Penny shook her head. "In fact," she admitted, feeling more than a little sheepish, "I may as well tell you —I, uh, didn't exactly have sex with him the other night, either."

"*Exactly*? What does *that* mean?"

Penny really did want to be as honest as possible, but… "It's complicated," she replied, pulling her arm away to straighten an already perfectly straight row of glasses on the shelving behind the bar and congratulating herself on having said something entirely truthful. "But all that really matters is that we didn't do it."

She feared Patti would be angry or hurt that she'd lied,

but when Penny looked back at her sister's eyes, they sparkled with happiness. "You made the right decision," she said, then grabbed back on to both of Penny's wrists. "And, oh my God, Pen, you and the hot computer babe! How did this happen? Tell me everything. And is it serious?"

Penny ignored everything else Patti had said except the last part since it stood out to her the most. She almost wanted to laugh at the very suggestion that it could be serious, since it was undoubtedly the most *un*serious, meaningless relationship she'd ever indulged—at least from his point of view, which kind of made her feelings irrelevant. But her heart hurt too much to even force any laughter, so she just attempted an easygoing expression. "No. In fact, he sort of dumped me already."

A look of horror reshaped Patti's expression. "What happened?"

Penny released a heavy breath, realizing she was sending her sister on a veritable roller coaster ride of emotion. "Martin is his boss. And Martin wants to marry me. You do the math."

"Oh," Patti said, catching on to the dilemma. "Oh, Pen, I'm so sorry."

Penny shook her head. "It wasn't important. Just a fling."

"You're lying again," her sister said without missing a beat. "You've never had a fling in your life—and besides, I can see it in your eyes. You've always been lousy at hiding your feelings."

Which meant…that Ryan had probably seen it last night, too—her hurt, her sadness.

But who cared anyway? She stiffened her spine, standing up a little straighter. Chemistry aside, who needed a guy that held her feelings in such low regard?

"Well, it looks like I've had a fling *now*. But I'm over it," she added—which wasn't entirely true, but no one needed to know that. And when Ryan showed up at her house this afternoon, she was going to fill him in, as well. The new and improved Penny she'd discovered last night after his departure was more than just wild—she was assertive, too, and she had no intention of putting up with this now-I-want-you, now-I-don't stuff. She planned to make her position clear, show him she wouldn't be walked on, and then he'd be sorry he couldn't have her.

Once more, Patti took Penny's hands, and now tried to look cheerful. "How about if Scott and I take you out to dinner tonight?" Penny could only guess that her firm independence had failed to show on her face just now, since her sister obviously felt sorry for her.

"Thanks, but I'll pass. I've always hated doing the third wheel thing."

"You wouldn't be a third wheel, I promise. And I want you to get to know him better."

Patti's current boyfriend had popped into the pub for lunch a couple of times, but Penny had never had the chance for more than a hello. "Why? Is *your* thing getting serious?"

Patti hedged a little, but resembled a bashful little girl when she finally smiled. "Kind of, maybe."

Penny gave her sister a quick hug, accompanied by a reassuring smile. "I'm glad. One of us should have a happy love life."

"Sure I can't talk you into dinner?" Patti asked again with a tilt of her head.

"Some other night, okay?"

She *did* want to get better acquainted with Scott—she couldn't remember the last time she'd seen her sister blush over a guy—but the timing was all wrong. Too much remained up in the air. Oh, she certainly didn't expect Ryan to stay at her house late again—in fact, she would make sure to get him out the door by five—but she wanted to be alone tonight in case Martin called. She wanted to close this crazy chapter of her life once and for all, then move on.

————

As she had for the past few days, Penny left the Two Sisters Pub just after the lunch rush, knowing Ryan would arrive around two. Upon getting home, the first thing she did was change into a pair of jeans—the rain had persisted and brought on a slight summer chill. Her Two Sisters T-shirt had gotten damp and limp from the rain, so she twisted the bottom into a knot, then swept her rain-frizzed hair high up on her head into a loose bun. The second thing she did was to stare at her phone for a minute, wondering what the heck was up with Martin's return phone call—or lack thereof. But staring didn't make the phone ring. Still no message, no Martin.

Next, she pulled up her system notes on the computer. She knew they would review whatever new screens Ryan had created first, but wanted to be ready to keep the work rolling. Just as she opened the pertinent file, the doorbell rang.

Taking a deep breath, ready to put all this foolishness with him to an end, she rose and whisked opened the door.

He stood on the front stoop, putting down his umbrella and looking just as handsome as ever. But she was going to ignore that completely. Holding the screen door open, she let him in out of the rain.

"We have to talk," he said, before even laying down his umbrella or taking off his trench coat.

"I agree." She crossed her arms.

"We can't keep doing what we've been doing. We can't keep…getting close. As in physically."

She let out a sigh of annoyance and rolled her eyes. "Yes, I think we keep agreeing on that, too."

But she suspected he hadn't even heard her since he rambled right on. "I'm thirty years old and dedicated to settling down and excelling in my career. And I've already been through my wild stage, and I just can't go there again, as much as I might like to. Okay?"

"Well," she said, just as directly, "I have news for you, too. I figured something out last night after you left."

"What's that?"

"It's that you're right. I *want* to be wild! I *want* to have fun! I want to do things I've never done before! And the last thing I need in my life is a man who can't deal with that. That means Martin *and* you."

Ryan's knees nearly gave out. She *wanted* to be wild now? And she wanted to get wild with someone other than *him*? Alarm raced through his body at lightning speed and his stomach clenched as images of her with another man flashed painfully through his mind. "Who, then? I mean… you're not just gonna go out and—"

"No, of course not!" she snapped—and relief chased the worry through his veins, but he still felt unsteady. "And it's not like I have some particular guy in mind, and it's not even like I'm on the hunt, for heaven's sake—but when I meet the right one, I'll know it. And *he* won't tell me how bad I am for him."

Ryan let out a huge sigh. He felt awful. And sort of sick. He'd thought he had this all figured out, thought he was going to come here, state his case, be completely sturdy and stalwart—even when desire struck—and then leave feeling like a new man.

Instead, he felt more like he'd been run over by a truck. The last thing he'd expected was to find out she didn't want him anymore. *And* that she was in the market for somebody else, somebody new—even if she'd claimed afterward that she wasn't.

Aborting his original plan, he ran a hand back through his rain-dampened hair, trying to summon the right words, trying to make up for everything he'd done wrong here. "I'm sorry I said that, about you being bad for me. I shouldn't blame you for my issues." He shifted his weight from one foot to the other, realizing that after all they'd been through in the few days they'd known each other, the least he owed her was some honesty. "But the thing is"—he met her gaze and lowered his voice—"I've never said no to myself on much of anything before. So I have to this time or else what kind of man *am* I? I can't keep screwing up my life for the sake of just following whims and doing what feels good at any particular moment." Oh hell, he wasn't saying this right. He needed to get to the heart of the matter, which was *her.* "But if I could, Penny…"

Her eyes changed then, looking like they belonged to someone much more gentle than the girl who'd just announced her sexual independence. "Yes?"

"Well, let's just say I'd give anything to help you explore this side of yourself, because it's a damn appealing side."

She swallowed visibly, appeared nervous. Dropped her gaze, but then raised it once more. "Really?"

He lowered his gaze, too, seeing for the first time that her feet were bare again, peeking from the bottom of her blue jeans. He nodded, and his groin began to tighten. Damn—just over her feet? But no—it was more than that. It was over all of her, every beautiful ounce of her. From her sweet, trusting eyes to the way her T-shirt hugged her breasts to the pale pink polish on her toenails. Part of him wished he hadn't said so much, been so honest, but he'd had to. He couldn't be so cold without at least letting her know why.

And it was in that moment of silence that Ryan finally understood the whole problem here.

When she'd seduced him in the limousine, he'd had no choice but to see her as some strong, bold, take-charge woman who wanted nothing more from him than a good time. Yet every moment they'd spent together since then had altered his thinking. She *was* that strong, bold woman —he knew it, he'd lived it. But she was also soft and vulnerable, the sort of woman who needed more than just the physical act of sex. And that part of her got to him. Down deep.

Maybe he'd almost begun to believe her when she insisted she wasn't wild, when she said the limo incident had been an aberration. But now she was changing her story again, telling him just the opposite, and he suddenly understood: She couldn't be labeled. It wasn't that simple, and it complicated every conflict inside him even further.

And yet, still more important was the fact that what he'd just said to her was so true: No matter who she was— June Cleaver or the sexy siren from the limo—he couldn't have her. Just couldn't.

"Have you talked to Martin yet?" he asked, just to say something.

"No. I called him, but he hasn't called back." She shifted her weight, the move jostling her breasts ever-so-slightly, and before he could stop himself, he wondered what kind of bra she wore under that T-shirt today.

"I'm sure he'll call soon."

"I hope so. I really want this thing with him settled. And this thing with *you* settled, too." Her resentful gaze shot through him and he could read it loud and clear. *You're not the guy for me. You're not the guy who'll give me what I need.*

Ah hell, he wanted to give it to her. And it seemed pure insanity that he'd turn down the offer of this beautiful woman to help her explore her sexuality, but she was right —the sooner it was settled, the better off they'd both be.

"I'm, uh, not gonna stay and work with you today," he said. "Sorry I didn't let you know sooner, but I didn't get much done this morning, so I don't have anything new to show you. I just came by to look at your CD drive like I promised."

He walked past her, not bothering to shed his raincoat since this would only take a minute. She followed, but he didn't look at her, just dropped to his knees upon reaching the desk, then took out the miniature toolkit he'd brought in his briefcase.

Removing the computer's cover, he wrangled and toyed with the wedged CD until it popped free. But one look into the empty drive told him it was shot. "It's broken," he announced.

"I knew that."

"I mean, I got the CD out, but if you put another one in, it'll stick again." Grabbing a notepad to write down the specifics about her computer, he added, "I'll order a new drive for you tomorrow, and I'll pick up a new modem, too."

She seemed taken aback by the offer. "You don't have to do that."

He still didn't look at her as he snapped the cover back into place and got to his feet. "I don't mind. Besides, I'm guessing most of your computer help has come from Martin lately, and you never know—after he hears that you're not gonna marry him, it might *never* get fixed."

She sighed. "You make a good point. Thanks...for the help."

He shook his head, at a loss for what else to say. But in his gut, he felt how easy it would still be to kiss her, and he smelled her damn shampoo again, even from a few feet away.

"I'd better go."

"Yes," she murmured. "You should."

Returning his tools to his briefcase, he snapped it shut, then picked up his umbrella. After pausing only long enough for one brief look into her pretty eyes, he headed for the door—but as he lowered his hand to the knob, he stopped and peered over his shoulder. "Penny, before I leave, I just have to know something."

"What's that?"

"The scent of your shampoo. What is it?"

"Uh...mango," she said, clearly bewildered. "Why?"

"No reason." He shook his head. "I just like it." Then he walked out into the rain.

Reaching the brick path below her porch, he put up his umbrella and trudged through the heavy drizzle toward the sidewalk that lined the quaint residential street. *Mango*. As fruits went, it struck him as a little exotic. Maybe even a little erotic. Kind of...wild. Just like the girl he was leaving behind.

He was really doing that, leaving her behind—Penny the Sandwich Girl, Penny the limousine seductress, Penny of the lavender bra. Pretty Penny.

Just put one foot in front of the other. You can do it.

But at the very thought of feet, hers came to mind. Why did he have to find them so sexy? Since when he a feet guy? Of course, he'd gotten a little peek at her belly button beneath her knotted shirt, too. Equally sexy, and not as bordering-on-weird for him to be aroused by. It seemed impossible that he'd seen so much more of her just last night and managed to walk out the door, yet today these little flashes of skin were making him nuts.

Just keep moving. You made it out last night, and you've made it out today, too. Piece of cake. Nothin' to it.

Though a disturbing image assaulted him as he trod up the sidewalk. It was Penny, back in the limo, but this time the lights were on. She was shedding her clothes, piece by delectable piece, before lowering herself into *another man's* lap, straddling him the way she'd straddled Ryan the other night. She gazed into the new guy's eyes, ran her hands through his hair, and whispered in his ear. *I want to be wild.*

Ryan swallowed, all too aware of the raging jealousy pulsing through his body. Jealousy for a guy who didn't even exist yet. Not to mention the nagging bulge that had grown beneath his pants. This woman was killing him. It wasn't even her fault, but she was driving him mad.

"Damn it," he muttered, stopping. He turned and looked back down the street, realizing he'd passed up his car, probably right around the time Penny had wiggled free of her panties in his mind. "Damn it, damn it, damn it."

He started back toward it, watching as it grew nearer through the rain, until he was almost there.

The only problem now was that he wanted her more than he wanted to breathe.

And he kept right on walking. Right past the car.

A moment later, he stood on her porch, one finger pressing down the doorbell, blood pumping through his veins like liquid heat. He didn't even have a plan. And didn't even care. Talk about following whims.

Penny pulled open the door and stared through the screen.

"I'm back," he said.

"Why?"

"I'm weak?"

Her eyes, a dark, misty shade of blue that somehow matched the rain, widened as she absorbed the unexpected. She'd come off pretty tough tonight, pretty stalwart, and he half expected her to tell him to go home—or maybe even to hell. He wouldn't blame her a bit if she did.

And when she just stood there staring at him, he told her the one thing he knew for sure. "And I'm not leaving this time."

Now her gaze narrowed on him, her expression turning a little bit sexy, a little bit sultry, and oh-so-inviting as she said, "Good, because this time I wouldn't let you if you tried." Then she bit her lip and reached for the door handle. "Now come in out of the rain."

Chapter Six

As Ryan stepped in from the chilling rain, the heat in her gaze hit him like a sledgehammer. Everything they'd done in the limo had been heaven on earth, but only now did he realize he hadn't been able to see her beautiful eyes then. The unspoken desire that shone in them now changed everything. And he was about to trade his entire career just for the look in those eyes, but at the moment, he didn't harbor even an ounce of regret.

His briefcase thudded to the floor and his wet umbrella followed. Without a word, he stepped forward to kiss her. Cupping her cheeks, his hands were gentle, but his kiss was not. Despite the rain, he felt like a man who'd just crossed a desert and as if she was his first drink of water.

When the kiss ended, she looked up at him, breath labored. "You're not holding anything back."

"What?" he murmured.

Her lips trembled. "That night in the limo, I could tell you were holding back. Even though you kissed me senseless, I knew there was more of you I wasn't quite getting."

"I was caught off-guard then. Hell, I'm always caught off-guard with you."

She curled her fingers into tight fists, crushing the fabric of his shirt within. "Don't hold anything back *now*, Ryan."

Her words swept through him like wildfire. "Don't worry, honey. I couldn't if I tried." And he meant it; he hadn't come back here to do anything halfway.

He lowered his mouth to hers again as she pushed the wet raincoat from his shoulders, his suit jacket with it. They fell to the floor in a heap behind him and she started working at his tie. His breath came heavy as his hands roamed up from her hips, grazing her breasts, his fingertips playing across the hardened peaks beneath her clothes to make her moan.

As he leaned her back against the wall, his aching erection pressed against the juncture of her thighs. She lifted to meet him, a slight, teasing grind at first, and then more urgent, until he lost himself in the hot friction. He kissed her with all the pent-up passion he'd harbored these past few agonizing days—it felt more like weeks, months—and his only thought was drinking in more of her.

When he finally pulled back from the kiss, their hips still locked in rough need, the wrenching passion in her eyes shot straight to his heart, and he suddenly understood something: This really mattered to her.

He'd known that before, known she was a woman who didn't take sex lightly, but maybe he'd underestimated her feelings. Yes, she was eager, hungry, but as he fell captive to the raw emotion on her face, he realized more than ever that this also had to do with her heart.

And while that might normally have had him pulling back, thinking twice, he couldn't pull away from Penny this time. He didn't have the power; her wringing need drew him like a magnet. And maybe that meant it mattered to him, too—but right now, he wasn't capable of thinking beyond this moment, and he wasn't even sure he *wanted* to look any deeper at his own response to the woman in his arms.

Unknotting her T-shirt, he pulled it off over her head to reveal a seductive powder blue bra that matched her eyes. Her breasts swelled from the hugging fabric, her rosy nipples visible through the lacy edge. "You're so sexy," he breathed.

Nuzzling her, he dropped a few soft, lingering kisses on her neck, shoulder, and was just about to use his teeth to ease down one bra strap when suddenly she clung tight to him. "Ryan, don't leave me this time."

The whispered words stunned him at first, but then his heart broke for every time he'd left her, even in the limo. He wished now that he'd stayed. "I won't. I promise," he answered, his voice strained, his chest tightening at his own words. This was surrender, total and complete.

Penny hated what she'd just said. First she'd so easily let her resolve be diminished, and now she felt as if she'd just given him that power she'd assumed when she'd let him back in, somehow shrinking back into her softer self. Yet when he'd returned to her doorstep, an almost paralyzing thrill had rushed through her, and now his touches had turned her weak. She'd told him the truth—she didn't want a guy who didn't want the same things she did—but saying it and sticking to it were two different things. What she felt with Ryan right now went beyond any normal sort of passion; it ran deep and boundless. Just as she'd feared last night, she cared for him. And she also feared that she'd just let him see it.

Still, though, he held her—he hadn't pulled away.

And more than that, he kissed her, slower now, his lips

playing gently over hers as his hands skimmed down her back and bottom.

When she finally unbuttoned his shirt and shoved it from his shoulders, one glimpse of his chest undid her. She'd felt its broad, smooth planes beneath her hands in the limo, had even seen it briefly after the light had come on, but now everything was different—every touch, every word, every glance went deeper.

"You're so beautiful," Ryan whispered, "that you make me ache."

The compliment spread all through her and she let it turn her wanton. "Don't worry. I think I can relieve that ache."

Okay, yes. This. Better. Not so weak just now. More in control. Taking control. That was who she wanted to be here. Just like in the limo. Just like in her mind when she let herself go there.

As he moved his hands to the button on her jeans, she pulled in her breath, her entire body tingling beneath the lust in his gaze. Part of her still couldn't quite believe she'd just said that, been so bold. Yet this was her, opening up completely, abandoning herself to brazen desire.

Then a knock came on the door.

Penny flinched and Ryan's fingers stilled. They exchanged startled looks and Penny's heartbeat kicked up another notch. This was just like the phone call last night, which had ruined everything. "I won't answer it," she whispered. "They'll go away."

As if on cue, though, the knock sounded again, this time accompanied by a voice. "Come on, Pen, I know you're home."

Penny pulled in her breath. "Oh no, it's Patti. And she's right. She knows I'm home. My car's outside and I'm supposed to be here...*working* with you."

Above her, Ryan let out a frustrated sigh. "Maybe we're working so hard we don't hear the doorbell."

She *wanted* to be working in the bedroom. Naked.

"I'll get rid of her," she said.

"Penny?" Patti yelled through the door, knocking again.

"Hurry," he whispered, the urgency in his voice shooting straight to the juncture of her thighs.

"Coming!" she called, and she was just about to break free of Ryan's embrace and grab up her shirt when the door burst open and Patti stepped in, Scott behind her.

"Scott got off work early and we decided to take in a, uh, matinee." Her smile froze on her face and Scott's eyes widened until they looked like they might pop from his head.

Penny and Ryan stood equally frozen in place and she wanted to die. Scott's gaze was glued to her and despite the fact that he'd probably seen a woman wearing a sexy bra before, he'd never seen *her* in a sexy bra. She could barely speak. "I *said* I was *coming*," she ground out between clenched teeth.

Patti's smile had now faded to the same horror-filled expression the rest of them wore. "Oops. I thought you said 'Come in.' Com*ing*, come in. They sound alike." Then she spoke more quickly, wringing her hands. "We just wanted to see if you'd changed your mind about meeting us for dinner later, but I'm guessing for sure now you haven't."

This time, Ryan answered for her. "Yeah, she'll be busy."

"Sorry," Patti said, backing out the door, stumbling into Scott, who now studied his shoes as he ran a hand uncomfortably back through his blond hair. "Bye."

As the door closed, shutting out the intrusion and the

sound of the still falling rain, Penny peered up at Ryan from a loose embrace.

"Now returning from the Twilight Zone," he said, looking nearly as dumbfounded as she felt.

"I can't believe that just happened." Her face burned hot from embarrassment. "I can't believe my sister's boyfriend just saw me half-undressed!"

And I can't believe this had to happen now, right when we were about to make wild, crazy, passionate love. Penny's heart sank as the expression on Ryan's face immediately overrode her concern about Scott. They'd been here before, after all, and she could guess what was coming. This would be the moment where he would change his mind, where he'd remember Martin and his job, where all the glorious heat they'd just been sharing would fall apart.

But instead Ryan simply pushed back a loose strand of hair from her face. "Oh, come on now," he murmured, "you're not really *half* undressed." He leaned near, their faces lingering close for a slow, sexy moment before he lowered his mouth to hers. She let the kiss melt down through her until finally she understood that she'd been wrong and this *wasn't* ending. This wasn't ending at all.

"To be half undressed," Ryan said, "this would have to be gone." He ran one finger down the strap of her bra. "Or, at the very least, these would have to come off." His touch returned to the front of her blue jeans and a wave of heat rushed through Penny's body. As he lowered the zipper, she quivered at the sensations underneath. He slid his hands inside, over her hips, pushing down the denim and giving a little growl as she wriggled free to reveal a skimpy swath of blue lace.

"Of course," he whispered, "we're not gonna stop at just the halfway point." He reached for her again, this time raining soft kisses on the exposed skin above her bra.

Lowering the blue straps until her breasts spilled free, he took one stiffened peak into his mouth, and she braced herself against the wall for support as his ministrations echoed through her. Oh, how she wanted this man, and she even somehow trusted him, so much, already. She'd never let a man get this close to her so quickly, but she found herself wanting to know all his secrets, his entire past, his dreams for the future, everything.

When he straightened, he cupped her face in his hands. "Tell me about your fantasies, Penny. Let me make more of them come true."

She bit her lip, nervous. Ryan was so sexy, and so comfortable and confident, that for a moment it frightened her. *But a few minutes ago you actually told him you could relieve his ache*—so she forced her nervousness aside. She wanted to be what she'd claimed to be—she wanted to be wild for him.

Trying to summon a reply, her thoughts flashed on the previous evening. "Last night after you left, I took a bath, and even though I was mad at you, I wished you were there. I..." Could she really say this part? "I imagined things...things you'd do to me in the tub."

Without prelude, Ryan bent to scoop her up in his arms, and carried her to the bathroom.

Soon he was running the water, adding bubble bath, setting the scene.

And despite herself, she panicked a little, because it had been one thing in the limo, in the dark, when she'd thought he was someone she knew, but this suddenly seemed like the *real* first time. They could see each other now. And they knew each other better. And for a life-long good girl trying to explore her naughty side, darkness and mystery had seemed easier than overhead lighting and being face-to-face in a bathtub.

"Wait right here," she said, an idea striking. Then she scurried from the room.

She wasn't sure this would take away her nervousness, but it couldn't hurt.

Two minutes later she returned to the bathroom carrying two wineglasses in one hand and a chilled, open bottle of Pinot Grigio in the other—and tucked beneath her thumb against the wine, a candle lighter for the few decorative candles already in the room. If ever there was a time to light the decorative candles, it was now.

Whisking back in she found Ryan already in the claw-foot tub, up to his waist in frothy bubbles. Oh my. The sight nearly took her breath away.

"So there was wine in your fantasy?"

She was honest. "No, but I'm a little nervous and wine relaxes me."

A half-grin turned up the corners of his mouth in response, and her heart beat harder as she set the glasses on the vanity and poured, all too aware of his eyes on her in her lacy lingerie. After that, she proceeded to light the candles, two near the sink and another on a low shelf by the tub. She handed him a glass of wine, took a sip of her own, then flipped off the light near the door, leaving the small room shadowy and aglow.

"There were candles then," he said with a playful glint in his eye.

She shook her head. "Nope. I'm adding them for ambiance. The fantasy is…still evolving."

His gaze on her narrowed. "I can work with that. Now take off your underwear for me before I lose my mind."

Whose fantasy is this? She almost said that but bit her tongue. Given that she wasn't quite as confident about taking control of this situation as she had been in the limo, or even a little while ago in the foyer, maybe she didn't mind if he called some of the shots.

Picking her wineglass back up, she took another sip, and then one more for good measure, feeling the instant warmth spread softly through her chest and letting it take away her inhibitions. "Hold this," she said then, passing him the glass.

And then—with the help of the wine and the candlelight and Ryan's sexy eyes—she became that other version of herself she was just starting to know. Giving her lower lip a soft, sensual bite, she reached behind her back with both hands, unhooked her bra, and slowly let it fall away, dropping to the tile floor at her feet.

A low groan echoed from Ryan's throat, the sound fueling her, adding to her excitement. Which made it easier to then push the blue lace from her hips down to her knees, until it lay at her ankles and she stepped free of it.

Standing before him entirely naked made her feel both vulnerable and desirable at the same time.

"You are so beautiful, honey," he said, voice deep. "And I'm so ready to live out another fantasy with you."

She carefully stepped into the tub, settling at the opposite end from him, their legs mingling beneath the water in a surprisingly comfortable intimacy. She'd actually never taken a bath with anyone else before, and as she took her glass back from the sexy man across from her, she thought she was going to like it.

He leaned back in the tub and gave her a slow, sultry smile. "So, last night, when you were thinking about us like this, what did I do to you?"

Her chest fluttered. But another sip of wine helped— even if her voice came out breathy. "You...used the sponge."

As his smile faded to a heat that radiated through her

body, he reached for the seashell-shaped sponge resting on the same shelf as the candle, along with a bottle of body wash. When he met her eyes in silent command, she understood what he wanted. One more sip of wine— before she set the glass aside and emerged from the bubbles, rising to her knees between his legs, the last remnants of her fear vanishing, finally chased away by the heat of anticipation.

He appeared deep in concentration as he swiped the sudsy sponge slowly across her stomach, arms, breasts, and she fell victim to the pleasure taking control of her body. When he drew it up the center of her in one long, luxurious stroke, her breath caught at the sensation, and something clenched tight deep in her womb.

"How am I doing?" he asked softly. "Anything like your fantasy?"

"Better."

"Tell me what happened next."

In reply, she lowered herself over his hips until she met his incredible hardness beneath the bubbles. Then she leaned near his ear and whispered the answer. "Sex."

Releasing a groan, he slid wet hands to her soapy bottom to guide her, and she sank easily onto him, although the sensation of being filled by him shook her to her very core. She remembered what having him inside her felt like from the limo, yet like all the rest of this, it seemed startlingly new.

Instinct made her move on him in slow circles, and she peered into his eyes the entire time, never looking away. She finally had that now, that glorious connection between their eyes even as their bodies connected below. Their gazes stayed locked until she shattered into a bliss that splashed water from the tub and left them both moaning with pleasure.

They didn't speak after that, but Ryan kissed her, slow and thorough, before helping her from the tub and grabbing a towel to wrap around her, then carrying her again —this time down the hall to her bed. The rainy day outside the windows kept the room dim and shadowed as he opened her towel and parted her thighs, kneeling in between.

"My fantasy now," he whispered, and bent to rake his tongue across her most sensitive spot, kissing and licking until Penny was biting her lip, lost to the tumult of sensation. She reached up to grip the wooden headboard until she was lifting herself against his mouth, moaning with each pulse of heat that swept through her. And when she came this time, it was harder, fiercer, making her clench her teeth and whimper until there were only sighs, hers and his, as he slid up beside her on the bed.

Gazing into his eyes, she realized how far gone she was. Frightening words echoed through her mind—*I love you.* She kept wanting to say them, but they couldn't be true, not this soon, not this quickly. She knew that. Yet it didn't diminish the emotion in her heart when she whispered, "Make love to me some more."

Rising up over her without delay, he placed his strong hands on her hips and entered her with ease. After a blissful sigh, she peered up at him and playfully observed, "This is the first time we've done it in a bed."

Fingertips curling possessively into her bottom, he gave her a gentle smile. "Probably not exactly the kind of thing you fantasize about, huh?"

Beneath him, she didn't answer, didn't tell him the truth that reverberated inside her.

Yes. Actually, it is.

With Ryan, it didn't take something wild to *feel* wild.

Or…maybe it was more accurate to say that *everything* with Ryan was wild.

———

WHEN PENNY AWOKE, they lay atop her comforter, a towel bunched beneath them, Ryan's arm looped around her waist. Raindrops still dotted the windows against a background of gray sky—darkness hadn't quite yet fallen. She turned to watch him sleeping, his head sharing a pillow with hers, and her entire body filled with warmth. Her heart nearly burst just watching him breathe, studying his dark eyelashes, noticing the lock of hair that fell over his forehead. Their sex had been the most thrilling, fulfilling experience Penny could ever remember.

Which was kind of scary, especially when she thought about their uncertain circumstances—but she didn't have time to deal with the worries, since at that very moment, he stretched and opened his eyes.

"Hi," she said.

He smiled. "Hi."

She swallowed, nervous. This was the aftermath, the moment when she'd find out if he regretted what they'd done. "How…are you?"

"Good," he said, then his grin turned rakish. "*Satisfied.*" He pulled her a little closer. "And you?"

"The same."

He kissed her forehead. "I like helping you live out your fantasies, Penny."

She let out a laugh as relief skittered through her. She'd been so afraid he'd regret it.

Just then, she heard his stomach growl. "Worked up an appetite, have you?" she teased him.

A light chuckle left him. "Actually, I've been thinking

about pot roast sandwiches, among other things, since I left here last night."

"Why don't I go whip a couple up and bring them back? It'll only take a minute."

"Hmm," he said, "dinner in bed. We could start a new trend."

Despite having offered, she hated pulling away from him, ending this perfect moment. But she had to be mature here—he knew this was only a fling, knew that was all it *could* be. So she couldn't act clingy and emotional...well, not any more than she perhaps already had in certain moments.

Grabbing a short, silky robe from a hook on her closet door, she headed for the kitchen and returned five minutes later carrying a tray laden with hot pot roast sandwiches, potato chips, and two cans of soda.

They ate, and talked, about anything and everything. About her business and more about her family, and about how he'd gotten into software design back in college. About childhood pets, places they'd been, local sports teams, favorite TV shows. Penny savored each and every moment, each nugget of information, every little insight into his soul. But she also wondered if this would be a one-time thing, and worried that they might never share such good, easy, gratifying communication again.

This must be what it's like for people who have flings. They lie around talking after sex—but then they go home afterward and it doesn't matter anymore. They see it as something pleasant, something fun, yet also no big deal. It didn't ebb its way into their souls like Penny could feel this discussion doing right now.

"I, uh, hope your sister wasn't in Martin's corner," Ryan said then.

Immediately understanding the implications, Penny quickly shook her head. "No, she's thrilled I'm not marrying him. In fact, I even told her about us—you and me—so walking in on us probably wasn't *quite* the shock it seemed."

"You told her about us?"

Oh, darn it, why had she said that? *This is what comes of getting too comfortable too fast—you screw things up.* "Well, not about the limo thing. Just that we were having a…" What were they having again? "A…thing. A fling." Yes, that was it.

Worry glimmered in his eyes. "She wouldn't tell—"

"Martin? Of course not. She understands the problem." And for the first time since Patti had left and Ryan had started taking off Penny's clothes again, she realized that even if Ryan didn't harbor any regrets about what they'd just done, there was a still a big issue to be dealt with. "Dare I, uh, ask about that problem? I mean, it's still there."

"To be honest," he said with a sigh, "I'm just not thinking about it right now."

And maybe she was crazy for even bringing this up, but she needed to know where they stood. "I was afraid after Patti showed up that you would change your mind again and leave."

"Well, *I'm* afraid," he replied, "that I probably couldn't have stopped if Martin himself had walked in."

The admission made Penny smile, but she tried not to think about the full extent of why, about all the emotions bubbling just beneath the surface of her calm exterior.

"The pot roast was great," he said then with a glance toward the empty plates on a large tray sitting between them on the bed. "Really hit the spot."

"I'm glad you liked it."

He dropped his eyes briefly before raising them back to

hers. "But I'd...better get going. Got a lot of work to do, you know."

"Oh," she said. "Yeah. Of course." She'd been hoping against his leaving, naturally, but waiting for it just the same. And it wasn't like he'd rushed right out the door after sex or anything—hours had passed. And he had to leave *sometime*.

Together, they rose from the bed and returned to the bathroom, gathering various clothes from the tiled floor. After stepping into his boxer briefs, he grabbed another towel to wipe up the water they'd splashed over the side— luckily, his suit pants had been dropped far enough away that only the cuffs had gotten wet. He raised his eyebrows and joked with Penny. "Good thing these survived the sloshing water. No telling what your neighbors would've thought if I'd had to go jogging out to my car in my underwear."

"I guess they'd have been onto me."

"Onto you?"

She hesitantly lifted her gaze, even as the warmth of a blush climbed her cheeks. "They'd realize I...have a secret wild side."

Ryan smile down at her easily, but she could've sworn it went a little deeper than what she'd just said, that he was seeing more of her than just the wild part. Or...maybe that was just a wish on her part. *And either way, wild girls who have flings shouldn't be reading too much into simple smiles when a guy is leaving. And wild or not, how on earth did I end up* having *a fling?*

Well, you thought it would be a good idea to seduce a man in the dark, that's how.

Lesson learned.

After he was dressed and she stood with him in the foyer, still in her flimsy robe, he lifted her hand to his mouth and softly kissed it. "See you tomorrow," he said with a smile. "We'll get back on track with our work then, keep moving forward."

She nodded, keeping her reply to herself. *Who cares about the stupid system?* Since she knew, all too well, that his job was important to him and she had to respect that. "Sounds good," she said instead.

"And Penny," he added, "me and you, in the tub, and the bed…"

Oh boy. Was this it? The other shoe dropping? Was he trying to tell her it couldn't happen again? "Yes?"

His voice went lower. "It was *phenomenal*. Thank God I had the sense to come back."

She said nothing, just letting the words wash through her. He might be leaving, but at least he'd left her with that.

He offered her a last smile, lowered a kiss to her forehead, and then turned to go, his coat draped over one arm, briefcase dangling from his other hand. Standing at the screen door, she watched him walk to his car. The rain had finally ended and the streets and sidewalk were already drying.

After closing the door, she made her way to the couch, where she plopped down and grabbed a pillow, hugging it in front of her. Joy and sorrow feuded inside her. Letting the joy win for a moment, she leaned her head back, reveling in the memories, in the realized fantasy that had been far more wonderful than anything she'd imagined, and in her true and utter abandon. Even though that part hadn't come quite as easy as she'd thought it would. *A learning curve.* But she'd pulled it off in the end, proving that her wild side was present and accounted for, and clearly open for business.

Yet then she bit her lip, wondering if it really counted

as being wild if you thought you might be falling in love. Maybe it wasn't wildness at all that she'd experienced today. Maybe it was just the beginning of something deeper.

She shook her head in disbelief. *Here you are, still trying to turn down one man's proposal, and you think you're already starting to fall in love with another?*

Well, that part wouldn't matter in the end anyway, since this was just casual sex to Ryan, and truly *couldn't* be any more than that as long as he remained at Schuster Systems.

She wasn't sure which was worse—knowing that, or *not* knowing how things would be between them tomorrow, and if they'd ever get wild together again.

Chapter Seven

"YOU'VE REACHED MARTIN SCHUSTER OF SCHUSTER Systems. Please leave a message."

Penny hung up the phone in the pub's office with a heavy sigh. Parts of her life were starting to play like a broken record. Which made her all the more thankful Ryan hadn't left before having sex with her last night—that was one pattern she'd been especially eager to alter. She got tingly inside every time she remembered it. Which meant she'd been tingling pretty much constantly since he'd walked out her door.

And as things with Ryan escalated, she burned with the need to talk to Martin, to get this proposal business cleared up. She glanced at her watch. Eight fifty-seven A.M. Almost six in Vegas. She'd thought certainly if she called him this early in the morning before the day's conference activities had begun, he'd answer.

Picking the phone back up, she redialed the Bellagio, and asked to be connected to his room. But still no answer. *This is getting ridiculous.* Of all times for Martin—Mr.

Dependable—to seem to fall off the face of the earth. She called the hotel again, and this time she asked the operator if she could have a message delivered personally to Mr. Schuster. "What's the message, ma'am?"

Simple. "Call Penny."

She couldn't believe it was Thursday, a week since she'd talked to him. But on the other hand, Martin always put the company first, so if there was some important early morning computer seminar, he'd be there. Or maybe he was having breakfast with potential clients or otherwise important contacts. Whatever the case, she could almost imagine his words when he finally got in touch with her. "Penny, I apologize for not calling, but I got so wrapped up in the conference that time got away from me." Then he'd drift into a tangent about the marvelous networking opportunities or the new technologies, mistakenly thinking she'd care.

"Hello, are you in there?" A brisk knock came on the office door as Patti's voice cut through her thoughts.

Penny swung the door open. "Hi," she said, but knew she sounded dejected.

"What's wrong? And why are you hiding in the office?"

"I was trying to get in touch with Martin, but no luck."

That was when Patti broke into a let's-tell-secrets smile. "Well, Martin's not the guy I want to hear about anyway. Tell me everything."

Penny wished she were more annoyed at her sister's nosiness, but it was kind of fun to be the one doing something exciting for a change. Even if she played aloof, tossing out, "Nothing to tell," as she sauntered past her into the pub.

"*Nothing to tell*," Patti mimicked, grabbing her wrist to spin her around. "Well, you can at least tell me where you got that bra. I thought poor Scott would have a heart attack."

Heat filled Penny's cheeks. "Me, too. I have no idea how I'll ever face the guy again. But I'm betting that's the last time you'll come barging into my house like that, huh?"

They both burst into laughter then, even if Penny's was laced with embarrassment. Her sister's eyes still danced with mirth, though, as she prodded, "Come on, Pen. At least tell me if he was good or not."

Penny cast a slow, wicked grin. "Well, he was…just as good as he looks like he'd be."

"Oooh, sounds fun." Patti took on a lascivious expression herself before pausing, seeming to size Penny up, and then giving her head a suspicious tilt. "So what's the deal with you anyway? Something's suddenly very different."

Her sister's powers of perception were truly amazing. But at least Penny still held her limousine encounter secret. It remained the one thing she was determined not to share. "What do you mean?"

"Oh, I don't have a word for it exactly, but…wow, Pen, having sex with a guy you hardly know? That's not like you. And in your foyer, too!"

"We didn't do it in the foyer," Penny cut in. But then she had to laugh at her own defensiveness as she added, "It was in the bathtub."

Patti joined in the giggling. "See what I mean? It's like you're a new woman."

"I kind of am," she confessed. "I've stumbled across a side of myself I never knew before." *Even if it's a side I'm still struggling to get comfortable with.* "A side that's letting me be a little more carefree and have a full-blown fling for once in my life."

"You lie," Patti accused, her tone shifting.

"What?"

"You keep using that word, *fling*—but new woman or not, I don't believe for a minute that's all this is. You as much as admitted that to me yesterday."

Penny sighed, but stood strong. "Be that as it may, a fling is all it *can* be, and I'm prepared to deal with that." *I think.*

"Oh, I get it," Patti replied. "You're really digging him, but he's still got this job hang-up going on."

"It's not a hang-up. Martin would probably fire him if he found out. At the very least, it would strain their relationship."

"Maybe he could get a *new* job," Patti suggested.

"Yeah, he could quit a good job he relocated for, so he can date a girl he barely knows. That makes a lot of sense."

"He had sex with you."

Twice, in fact, although Patti didn't know that part. "A lot of people have a lot of sex without quitting their jobs over it. I don't think he feels obligated to me just because I invited him into my bathtub."

She hated the look that formed on her sister's face because it said so much without saying a word. Things like *I feel so bad for you*, and *I can see you're crazy about him*, and *You're gonna get your heart broken.*

"Don't worry," Penny insisted, "I can handle this." Besides, she had no other choice. She'd let herself go wild with him, and she hadn't asked for promises. "For all I know, it won't even happen again. And if so...I'll live." *Even if I'm miserable for a while.*

When the phone rang, she flinched, thinking it was Martin, and raced to snatch up the receiver. "Two Sisters Pub. This is Penny."

"Hi Penny, it's Grace."

She suppressed a groan—Martin was still MIA. "Hi Grace. What's up?"

"I want to place a breakfast order."

"Breakfast, huh?" She tried to sound light-hearted. "That's different." Schuster Systems ordered five to ten lunches from them every day, but never breakfast.

"I know"—Grace laughed—"but Eve, Ryan, and I were standing here saying how hungry we are, and we decided some danishes sounded good. We want two apple, two cheese and one cherry."

Penny scribbled the order, but was stuck back on hearing Ryan's name, on envisioning him standing at Grace's desk this very second, listening to their phone call. "Got it. Anything else?"

"No, that's it. I'll be down in five to get them."

"I can bring them up," Penny offered.

"Are you sure?"

"I'm not busy, so why not?"

After she got off the phone, she packed the order and told Patti where she was headed. Her sister simply shook her head. "Fling, my butt."

"I'm not going up there just to see *him*. I'm going...to be nice." And that was partially true. She and Grace were casual friends and she knew Grace was busier than she was this time of day, answering phones and dealing with early morning office duties. In fact, that's how the daily sandwich delivery ritual had originally begun. Grace had been unable to leave the phones for several days in a row at lunchtime, and Penny had offered to start bringing the lunch order up.

When she stepped off the elevator a few minutes later at Schuster Systems, everything felt normal. The lobby's polished wooden trim shone beneath recessed lighting, and fresh flower arrangements adorned the tables in the small waiting area. Grace resided behind her circular desk, her hair swept back in its usual bun, and she looked buried in mail-sorting. Penny approached with a smile. "Two apple, two cheese, one cherry," she said, handing over the white bag.

Grace pushed up her stylish glasses. "That was quick."

Penny shrugged. "Five danishes are easier than five sandwiches."

Just then, Ryan passed through the rear of the lobby behind Grace's desk, a handful of CDs clutched in his fist. He glanced up, saw Penny, then stopped short. "Uh, hi."

And suddenly nothing felt very normal anymore. Her heart nearly stopped at the sight of his smile on this official "morning after," and she almost smiled back, but then remembered that Grace was sitting right there. "Hi," she said, trying to sound completely casual. "I...brought your danish."

He seemed to catch on then, his eyes flashing just a hint of collusion. "Great. Thanks."

"I'll bring it back to you in a minute," Grace told him over her shoulder.

"Thanks," he said again, then gave Penny a quick wink before heading on his way.

"So," Grace said when he was gone, "I bet you're looking forward to Martin's return in a few days."

Penny winced inside, then drew her gaze down to the receptionist's friendly eyes. "Uh, yeah." *For more reasons than you know.* Then she tilted her head, taking the opportunity to ask, "Grace, have you heard from Martin since he's been away?"

Grace shook her head. "No, but that's not uncommon. He's such a workaholic, he tends to get so mired in whatever he's doing that he forgets to check in. And he trusts me to keep things moving smoothly while he's gone." A hint of pride echoed in her voice.

"Then you don't think it's a little weird that I haven't heard from him, either?"

She tilted her head. "Not really. He's probably backing off, trying to give you some space, time to think."

Penny knew Martin had told Grace about his proposal before he'd left. Grace had been with him since Schuster Systems' inception and he tended to share certain personal issues with her as a matter of course.

"That would make sense," Penny said, "except that I've left tons of messages for him."

Grace gave her an encouraging look. "I wouldn't worry, Penny. It's like I said. He's probably completely immersed in conference activities and hasn't even checked his messages. Those events can be really hectic and tiring."

Penny nodded, reassured if not consoled. "Yeah, that's what I was thinking, too."

"But I'm sure you're on his mind every second." Grace smiled. "I'm sure he's hoping to slip a ring on your finger as soon as he gets back."

That's the part that's eating me alive. But of course she kept that to herself and just said, "Thanks, Grace," before stepping back onto the elevator.

———

RYAN FELT great as he moved up Penny's front walk. He *shouldn't* feel great—he knew that. He should feel awful. And it wasn't that he'd quit worrying about Martin and his job—but damn, yesterday with Penny had been incredible. A dart of pleasure arced through him just remembering.

When he looked back on his life, he couldn't remember ever knowing anyone like her. He'd dated mostly sophisticated girls, or at least girls who *thought* they were sophisticated—cheerleaders in high school, sorority girls in college, and since then, other white-collar types like himself. Or he'd *thought* they were like him, anyway. But something in those relationships had always lacked...what? Heart? Substance?

He'd probably talked more with Penny in the short time he'd known her than he ever had with any other woman. It had happened again after they'd had that amazingly hot sex yesterday. They'd just talked. About everything. And nothing. It had been nice. So nice that leaving hadn't come as easy as he would have liked, but he'd done it anyway because it had seemed the prudent thing to do. If he could call anything about yesterday afternoon prudent.

So for now, he had no answers; he just had to go with the flow. The good news was that he'd gotten a tremendous amount of work done on her system last night. Relieving his sexual frustrations with her must have been good for him on more than one level.

When she whisked open the door, she wore short denim shorts that hugged her slender hips and a bright red tank top that conformed to her curves as well. Her sandy-blond hair cascaded over her shoulders as she said, "Hi."

The very sight of her left him speechless. After all, this morning at the office she'd been wearing her typical T-shirt and baseball cap—which was cute, but now she just looked plain sexy. "Uh, hi," he finally sputtered, then realized his gaze rested on her chest. He yanked it to her face, and then laughed at himself, knowing full well she'd seen where his eyes had been. "Sorry. But you look good."

She gave him a bashful smile. "Thanks."

Ah yes, the simpler Penny. The innocent, down-to-earth-kinda-sexy girl-next-door Penny. But he knew what lay underneath that innocent veneer, and the mere knowledge drove him crazy. He wasted no time stepping closer, sliding his arms around her waist, then lowering a kiss to her lips that heated his blood. As she pressed her palms warmly to his chest, he purred in her ear, "So tell me, what kind of bra are you wearing today?"

A coquettish look formed in her pretty eyes. "Wouldn't you like to know." Mmm, the vixen Penny had arrived.

Lifting a hand to her shoulder, Ryan eased a fingertip beneath her tank top to reveal an equally red strap. His heart stopped. "Nice. Can I see the rest?"

"Now?" She looked amused.

So he let his eyes fall briefly shut and let out a sigh. "You're right. We have to work, don't we?"

"Not that I don't find you tempting," she confessed, biting her lip in that provocative way he loved, "but working would probably be a good idea, since we didn't yesterday."

Though it required a few deep, fortifying breaths on this part, to his surprise he actually found backing away from her a little easier now, likely because he knew there would be more, and because he no longer had to pretend nothing was going on between them. In one sense, he knew falling into this relationship was insane, but he'd surrendered to her yesterday in a way he couldn't ignore. When Martin came home...well, they'd deal with that then. But for now, things felt too damn good to worry about the future.

"My computer was finally delivered to the office today," he said, taking a seat at her desk. "While the wholesale guy was there, I ordered your CD drive and modem."

"Thank you," she replied with a warm smile, walking over to place one hand on his cheek.

He grinned uncertainly. "It's only a couple of computer parts."

"No, that's not what I mean. Thank you for that, too. But what I'm really thanking you for is…kissing me hello. I was afraid of how things would be when you arrived today, afraid you'd come in here telling me we can't 'get close' anymore, afraid things would've changed overnight."

Ryan shook his head and admitted to her what he'd been forced to admit to himself. "I think I've proven I have no self control where you're concerned. I've given up."

She grinned. "A man at my mercy. I like that."

"Be gentle," he begged, teasing.

After another kiss, though, he forced his attention to her computer, making a couple of clicks of the mouse.

"What are you doing?"

"Reinstalling your printer," he said, finishing the short process with a few keystrokes, and then standing up to let her have the chair. "Why don't you pull up your system notes and see if it works."

A moment later, the printer kicked to life and Penny's notes started filling the white pages that pushed through it. "Great," she said.

Frankly, Ryan found it unbelievable that Martin couldn't have taken care of something so simple for her, or at the very least suggested she try reinstalling herself. Clearly, the guy hadn't even spent five minutes on the problem. "You know what this means, don't you?" he asked.

"What?" She snatched up some pages from the printer tray as if they were the most amazing things she'd ever seen.

"We don't have to confine ourselves to working here anymore." Of course, as recently as yesterday, his plan had been to make sure they started working in the office instead, but things had changed since then. "It's a beautiful day outside," he went on. "Yesterday's rain cooled things down. And I've heard a lot about Eden Park since I got here, but I haven't had the chance to check it out, even though it's just up the hill from my condo. So what do you say we take your notes and my laptop and get out in the sunshine?"

Her smile returned. "When do we leave?"

"How about as soon as your notes finish printing? I stopped by my place and threw some shorts in my briefcase, so I'll need to change."

"And I'll need my flip-flops," she added.

Ryan headed to the bathroom to shed his suit, but he got a bit sidetracked upon stepping back into the romantically retro little room where he and Penny had been so intimate just yesterday. They were so damn good together, when he let them be, that it kind of…filled him up inside. He didn't know what it filled him up *with* precisely, and he wasn't inclined to examine it too closely, but he knew he liked it, and that he wasn't any more ready to let it go than she was.

When he exited a minute later in khaki shorts and a T-shirt, he found Penny in her bedroom, pulling her hair into a ponytail at the nape of her neck. "Almost ready?" he asked. The printer had quieted in the other room.

She swung open a closet door. "Just need my shoes. Can you shut that drawer for me?" She pointed over her shoulder at an antique chifforobe just behind him. "I must have left it open this morning when I was getting out *this*." She reached inside her tank top to playfully flash the strap of the red bra, teasing him with raised eyebrows before turning to the closet.

"Sure." Bending to push closed a drawer that appeared to be filled with a tempting rainbow of bras, he realized the drawer underneath it was open a little as well. As he reached to shut it as well, his eyes fell on cotton panties—and something even far more interesting than her lacy lingerie. He followed the gut instinct to open that drawer wider to take a better look. Make sure he was seeing what he thought he was seeing.

He stopped breathing when he spied—yep, and wow—a pair of heart-shaped handcuffs covered in red velvet. And he'd thought she was wild before? This gave a whole new meaning to the word.

Then again, this *was* the same girl who'd seduced him in a dark limousine.

He didn't hesitate to grab them up and turn toward her, clearing his throat.

When she spun to face him, the handcuffs, which still sported a tag, dangled from one fingertip. "Victim of Love Handcuffs for Lovers?" he asked with one arched brow.

Her jaw dropped like a stone and he couldn't deny enjoying her stunned expression. "That was a—a gag gift. My sister gave them to me, for some insane reason"—she gesticulated wildly—"on my twenty-fifth birthday."

"Twenty-fifth, huh? How long ago was that?"

"Almost four years."

He grinned. "Keeping them handy for some reason?"

She continued to look mortified, and he mischievously took pleasure from it—until she finally let out a huge sigh. "Okay, fine, you caught me. I was cleaning out the basement a few weeks ago and found them. And I guess I was sort of saving them just in case…well, you know, in case Martin…"

"Had a wild side," he finished for her.

She nodded, her pretty face nearly as red as the top she wore. "Now can we just go, please?"

Aw hell—she looked so distressed that it was starting to take the fun out of this. So he

dropped the handcuffs on the bed with a sign and came toward her. Even though it had been fun for a minute, he didn't want her to be embarrassed about a side of her that was so fun, and so damn enticing. "Penny," he said, "it's okay. And I'll be happy to help."

"Happy to help with *what?*" she asked, exasperated.

He winked and pulled her into a warm embrace. "Trying the cuffs out later."

———

PENNY HAD WANTED to die when Ryan pulled those velvet handcuffs from her drawer. She'd forgotten they were even there, and now regretted putting them someplace so accessible. Of course, at the time, she'd actually thought she'd *wanted* them accessible, just in case anything interesting ever transpired with Martin. But thinking about that now made her want to throw the dumb things in the garbage as soon as she got back home.

Thankfully, though, Ryan had been merciful enough not to mention them again and now they shared a lovely afternoon. First, they'd stopped at a shop in Mt. Adams to grab some wine and fruit to snack on. Ryan had also plucked up a small bouquet of daisies from a stand of flowers, handing them to her with a wink as he told the shopkeeper to add them to the bill. He couldn't know how the small gesture had melted her heart, but she still held the flowers now, even as she lay on her stomach on the blanket they'd spread next to the pond at the overlook.

Most people came to this particular spot for the view of the Ohio River wending its way through the valley below, but Penny loved the garden atmosphere, the old picturesque bridge that crossed the stream leading from the pond, the large shade trees that left the grass dappled with sunlight.

"This is a nice place," Ryan said, looking up from his laptop to watch a few kids run across the bridge.

She lay next to where he sat, facing the other way, so she twisted her neck to see. "Yeah, I come here a lot," she replied. "Lately, with Martin."

"Oh." Ryan's smile disappeared. "So then this is kind of a…special place. For you and him."

Penny sighed and snapped a grape from a bunch lying on a napkin between them. "No, not really. And as I'm realizing more every day, nothing with Martin was actually all that special. It was more like…two *friends* going to the park together. Two *buddies*."

She popped the grape in her mouth and stopped short of telling Ryan that this, today, being here with him, was special. In fact, she found herself noticing the park's details in a way she never had before. She'd never really seen the ducks' wakes spreading across the water, or the vibrant purple flowers that jutted from the garden to their right, or the cheerful old men with their remote control riverboats, one sporting a calliope that played even now. Oh, she'd *seen* all of it before, but maybe she'd never really felt it, absorbed it, the same way she was right this moment.

"Grape, please," Ryan requested, but his eyes were locked on the screen and he typed furiously. She pulled another from the bunch and lifted it to his lips—and he leaned to take it with his mouth, along with her finger, which he slowly sucked from base to tip before letting go.

As an unexpected bolt of pleasure shot through her, a barely there moan escaped her.

"That's just a taste of what's to come later," he

promised with one of his devilish grins, "if we can get back to work."

On that note, they dove back into the project in earnest and finished reviewing the screens Ryan had created since yesterday. There were a lot, more than she could have imagined a single person designing in less than a day. "I can't believe how rapidly this is going," she said. "I thought it would take weeks to get to this point."

"Usually it might, but I guess I'm a pretty fast worker when I'm into what I'm doing." She found his boyish modesty appealing. "Of course, it'll be a while before all this is fully testable. What I'm showing you now is just to see if we're on the same page before I get it all tied together and functional. And besides, the lengthy part will be the menu and cashiering systems."

But Penny barely heard the last part, because—oh boy. She couldn't believe what she was seeing. Was that Grace in the distance? Grace had a cute Scottish terrier just like the one on the woman's leash, and the woman had the same hair color and build.

Before Penny could utter a word, the woman in question turned her head, and sure enough, it was Grace.

"Uh-oh."

"Uh-oh what?" Ryan asked absently, still focused on the screen.

"Grace is here. Up on the sidewalk by the street."

The announcement got his full attention; he stopped typing to sneak a glance over his shoulder, then dropped a dread-filled gaze to Penny. "What on earth is she doing here?"

"Walking her dog."

"No, I mean, why isn't she at work?"

Penny checked her watch. "It's almost six."

He shook his head with a sigh. "Damn it, woman, you make me lose track of time."

Penny would have liked to enjoy the remark more, but unfortunately Grace's dog had just frolicked off the walkway into the grass, coming closer. Penny pulled in her breath and spoke lowly. "Don't look now, but Snowy is hunting for the perfect place to relieve himself, and he's heading our way."

Chapter Eight

Ryan couldn't believe his rotten luck. He didn't know much about the inner workings of Schuster Systems yet, but he'd already figured out that Grace was Martin's right hand around the office. "What are the chances?" he murmured, incredulous. "Of all the parks in the city, she has to choose *this* one?"

Penny ducked her head behind him just slightly, then peeked around his shoulder. "Grace lives in Walnut Hills, just a few blocks from here."

He sighed, then muttered, "Great."

"I've never actually seen her here, though," she said, lifting a wary gaze. "I didn't even think about her living so close. Sorry."

He nodded, trying to relax. "It's not your fault."

"Don't look so worried. After all, we're not actually doing anything wrong. We're working. You have a computer and you're keying stuff into it as we speak."

Keeping his voice low, he pointed out, "Penny, I don't think most system designers lie on blankets in parks with their clients while they work. With fruit and wine and flowers, no less."

Just then, though, a smile stretched across her face when he least expected it. He didn't want to take the chance of turning his head to see why, so he asked, "What is it? What's happening?"

"She's leaving."

He flinched in surprise. "She is?"

"Snowy didn't find the right spot, I guess." Her tone was less furtive now. "He's back on the sidewalk and they're moving past, headed for home."

At this, he let out the huge breath he didn't even realize he'd been holding.

"I don't think she saw us," Penny added, reaching one hand to his knee, and the touch heartened him.

He finally looked over his shoulder to see for himself, and sure enough, he caught a last glimpse of Grace and her little white dog just before they disappeared from view behind a stand of small trees. Real relief finally washed over him then—but he didn't like hiding from a woman they both liked, a woman he knew considered Penny a friend.

"Would you be disappointed," he asked, "if I suggested we call it a day and get the hell out of here before the dog changes his mind and brings her back?"

"Not at all." Penny's tone sounded sincere, and he hoped it was, because he didn't want her to feel like they were doing something wrong. It would be great if he could just ditch this job for her, but it wasn't that easy, even as much as he hated the idea of sneaking around. Shutting his laptop, he decided to change the subject and lighten things up.

"Though I have to admit," he teased her, "I'm gonna

miss the great view you've been giving me down your top all afternoon."

Her gaze dropped to the cleavage that had been visible ever since she'd rolled onto her stomach. Looking back up, her pretty blue eyes widened on him as she smacked his thigh.

"Oh, into the rough stuff, huh? First handcuffs, now whips and chains?"

"Hey!" She rose to her knees in a show of mock outrage. "You'd better watch it."

"Or what? You'll use them on me?"

A playful chase ensued as Ryan hopped to his feet and dashed behind an old maple tree, Penny following. When he let her catch him, they both toppled softly to the grass, his arms falling around her waist. Her pretty eyes, her pretty mouth, lay so close that he couldn't keep from kissing her—a kiss that was short and sweet, but whisked through him like fire. Afterward, their eyes met and the moment turned slow, heated, that fast. Ryan's heart beat too hard and he wondered how the mood had turned so serious again that quickly.

"Uh, what happened to getting out of here?" he said, wishing his voice didn't sound so husky.

"I don't know." Hers sounded just as breathy, just as sexy.

"We should do that," he managed, gently urging her up off of him, then getting to his feet as well.

"Right," she murmured. Although she still looked equally as taken with him as he was with her. Time to make things light again—fast.

He smiled and raised his eyebrows. "Race ya." With that, he headed back to their blanket, and soon ran toward his car lugging his briefcase, and a corked half-empty bottle of wine. Penny hurried behind, toting the flowers and a mini brown shopping bag packed with leftover fruit and plastic cups, much of the old quilt she'd brought dragging after her.

Throwing their things into the backseat, they both got into the car breathless, although he had beaten her by a mile. "You're gonna have to be a little faster," he said with a wink, "if you intend to catch me with those lovecuffs of yours."

"Watch it," she warned, and she smiled, but her sudden blush told him that maybe he'd just taken the joke a little too far, again.

"I'm only teasing, honey," he said, lifting her chin with one bent finger.

And as he looked into those sweet, innocent eyes of hers, he realized that she truly was just as shy as she was wild. The unlikely combination twisted Ryan's heart in a way he never could've foreseen a week ago.

"Come here." He leaned over the gearshift to kiss her, a kiss he wished would show her it didn't matter to him *what* she was—pure as the driven snow or wild as the night —but that he just liked being with her.

She returned the kiss with a warmth that tightened his chest.

"Mmm," he said when it ended, "I wasn't teasing about that, though. I say we grab some dinner, then go back to your place." He flashed a grin designed to tempt.

"On one condition."

"Anything."

"No more mention of the red velvet you-know-whats."

He dropped a quick kiss on her forehead before easing back in his seat. "You got it."

It was only as Ryan maneuvered the meandering drive that led back to the main road, though, that he realized Penny hadn't thrown *everything* she'd been carrying into the back. The daisies he'd given her remained lying across her lap.

And maybe that meant nothing—maybe it just meant she liked flowers. Yet another glance made him think she was holding on to them like something special, something...cherished. Hell, he'd determined before that she took sex pretty seriously, which had to mean she was taking *them*—him and her—seriously, too. Didn't it?

Well, like the Martin issue, he couldn't think about that now. It was another thing not to examine too closely, another thing to push out of his mind because it made a difficult situation easier to handle.

Just enjoy her. Enjoy what's going on between you. Just live for right now and don't start thinking about her heart.

And whatever you do, don't start thinking about yours, either.

———

HOURS LATER, Penny gazed up at Ryan in bed.

Candles provided the room's only light as she lay beneath him in only a pair of panties. She could see the clear outline of his erection through his boxer briefs, but enjoyed studying the rest of him, too: his broad shoulders and muscular arms, the light dusting of hair on his chest, the hungry look in his eyes as he watched her.

"Wanna do something exciting?" he suggested.

She bit her lip, a bit nervous as usual at such times, yet infused with the boldness that had brought her this far into the most thrilling relationship of her life. "What do you have in mind?"

"Do you trust me?"

The question caught her off guard. "Yes. Why?"

He answered by gently raising her arms above her head, dropping a kiss on her waiting lips, then closing

143

something around both her wrists before she even knew it. Leaning her head back on the pillow, she glanced up to see the heart-shaped handcuffs, the silver chain that connected them circling one of the wooden bed rails. She gasped, then looked back to him. "You promised…"

"Not to mention them. I haven't. And I won't."

She met his gaze in the candlelight, not quite sure what to think. "But how did you…?"

"I snuck in here a little while ago and hid them under the pillows."

"You really mean to lock me up?"

"I just did." He kissed her again. "Is that okay?"

Penny didn't know what to say. Her heart beat out of control. She wasn't even really sure what pleasure people derived from this, yet on the other hand, adventure beckoned, even if only timidly. "I…I guess."

"Look at it this way, honey," he whispered. "It only means I want to be the one to do all the work here, and give you all the pleasure. I want to make you feel things. Hot, incredible things."

Well, *that* sounded impossible to resist. So she didn't.

And it *was* an act of trust. Because, of course, letting someone handcuff you meant they could do anything they wanted to you, leaving you powerless to stop them. But she liked the way he'd framed it—that it only meant he wanted to control the pleasure he delivered, and that was…well, undeniably hot.

And minutes later, as he rained scintillating kisses over every inch of her body, she came to understand *exactly* what pleasure people derived from this. Placing herself under his control felt somehow primal. And as an independent woman, a part of her wanted not to like it—but some things were as old as time, as natural as breathing, and maybe wanting to give yourself so wholly to a man was one of them. Yes, it required a complete and abiding trust. And now she knew why he'd asked—and oh yes, she trusted him, more in this moment than ever before.

Of course, she remained plagued by the part of her that couldn't quite let go of Pretty Penny, the part that said, *What on earth are you doing?* But the pleasure overrode her good girl doubts enough that she could close her eyes and stop thinking, stop reasoning, long enough to just *feel*.

She wasn't sure when she became aware that the velvet cuffs were actually too loose, that she could slip her hands free if she wanted. But she ignored the knowledge and never let Ryan know, instead continuing to bask in all the sweet and tantalizing things he did to her with his mouth and hands.

And just when he'd driven her to the brink of insanity —he reached above her head and freed her wrists, letting the soft handcuffs drop to the hardwood floor. After which he made love to her in the low glow of the candles, starting out scintillatingly slow with deep, lingering strokes—until their movements gradually edged into something rougher and more urgent.

They both lay recovering afterward, half asleep and entangled in each other's arms, when he whispered an accusation in her ear. "You can tell me you never fantasized about playing with those cuffs, but I know you did."

Without opening her eyes, she smiled and murmured the truth in his ear. "It was just like the bathtub."

"What do you mean?"

"Better than I thought it would be."

―――――

RYAN RESTED on Penny's overstuffed couch, the candles from the bedroom having been brought out to keep the room dimly lit. At the other end, Penny sat with her knees curled beneath her, her short, silky robe draping her body. Ryan wore only underwear as they made a mismatched late-night snack of grilled cheese sandwiches, tortilla chips, and wine. Penny had offered to cook something more, but Ryan hadn't wanted to put her to any trouble, so they'd scavenged for whatever was quick and easy.

Beyond the windows and doorways, everything lay black and silent, and it seemed as if the whole world was this room, he and Penny the only people in it. *That would simplify things.*

He drew his gaze from the flickering shadows on the walls down to the woman across from him. He felt closer to her with each passing hour, with each moment he held her, touched her, absorbed more of the sweet honesty in her eyes.

And before this was over, he was going to hurt her. He knew it without a doubt.

He didn't want to think about that, but the darkness had somehow forced it to surface. What they had, no matter how good, couldn't last forever, and probably not even for much longer. In the end, he would jilt this beautiful, sexy, vibrant, sincere woman…for a job.

But wait. Not just a job. A career. His last shot at doing something substantial and fulfilling.

"What are you thinking about?"

His eyes had drifted back to the shadowy patterns of light dancing across the wall, but he lowered them to find Penny setting her empty plate and wineglass aside to move closer to him on the couch. As she snuggled up with him, he soaked up her warmth…and felt far too serious.

He didn't do that a lot, get serious with women—he wasn't crazy about letting his vulnerabilities show. But then, he supposed she'd already seen those vulnerabilities, more times than he could count. *So hell, why not just do what* she *would do if he asked her the same question? Why not just be honest?*

Well, *sort* of honest, anyway. "I'm thinking about where I've been and where I've come to." That stuff had been on his mind, as well—and it would be a whole lot easier than telling her he knew he was going to hurt her.

Her solemn eyes seemed to carve a path to his soul. "I know where you've come to, but I don't know the part about where you've been."

He hesitated, trying to decide if he really wanted to talk about that, his life up to now, but then he realized he did. Because it might help her understand better when this ended. Or…maybe it just felt good to be with someone who really wanted to get to know him better, someone who cared. "I grew up in rural Indiana," he began, "home of basketball and Bible meetings."

"Did you play? And did you go?"

He grinned. "No, and no. I was the family non-conformist, the one who stood out like a sore thumb. Now my older brother, Dan, on the other hand, was the captain of the basketball team, led the youth group at church, and just for good measure, was named valedictorian of his senior class. Me, I was a good kid, but I still fell short of the mark, you know?"

She cast a sympathetic look. "Actually, no, I'm afraid I don't. Patti would probably relate, though. We were both good kids, but I was a little more…um, flawless, I guess you might say."

He offered a wry grin. "Ironic that I would end up with the perfect one."

"Well, maybe I've been a little less perfect lately."

Ryan shook his head. "I would disagree."

They shared a warm smile until she said, "So how are things with your family now?"

He shrugged. "I'm still the non-conformist—I moved away to a white-collar world instead of staying in blue-collar Akinsville, Indiana. But I send home money every month because they're retired now and they need some financial help, and it's a way I can sort of…give back whatever they didn't get from me as a son."

"Ryan, I'm sure they love you and think you're a great son."

He smiled in concession. "Okay, maybe I got a little melodramatic there. Of course they love me. But I'm not sure Dan doesn't make them just a little happier than I do." He ended with a wink, trying to make the sentiment sound lighter than it actually was.

"And just where did the basketball-playing, Bible-toting valedictorian end up?"

"Right where any good basketball-playing, Bible-toting valedictorian should. Still in the heart of our hometown. He teaches English at the high school and coached the basketball team to the state championship last year. He married a perfect woman and they live in a perfect little house with two perfect children and a perfect dog. On the weekends, they drive an hour and a half to Indianapolis to do volunteer work at a homeless shelter. Carol serves up food while Dan teaches illiterate people to read."

"Wow."

He flashed a cynical look. "See what I mean? He's a hard act to follow."

"Still, Ryan, your parents have to be proud of you. Look at you—working on the cutting edge of technology, making enough money that you can send some home. It's a wonderful accomplishment."

"More wonderful when you can hold on to your jobs."

"What?"

Damn, what was he doing? Aw hell, just telling her more of the truth, and she deserved to hear it. This, too, would help her better understand why this had to end when the time came.

"The fact is, Penny, the reason I'm here—in Cincinnati, working for Martin—is because he liked me enough not to ask for references." From there, he went on, telling her what had happened at ComData, and before that at Futureware. He meant to give her the short versions, but her eyes shone with such understanding that he ended up sharing the longer ones. And he expected to feel humiliated when he finished, but he didn't.

"Anyway," he concluded, "that's why this job means so much to me. It feels sort of like…a last chance. A last chance to make my parents proud and convince them I can handle the path I chose, and a last chance to make *myself* proud, too."

"Ah, now that part I can relate to." She reached for her wineglass and took a sip. "I felt directionless when Patti and I decided to open the pub. If it had failed, I wouldn't have known where to go, what to do, who I'd become. Before that, I'd wandered aimlessly from job to job, and I wanted more, something concrete and lasting. And even though I didn't have issues with my parents, I still wanted to make them proud."

"So maybe you understand a little more now about trying to settle down, wanting to walk the straight and narrow."

"Yeah," she said, a slight look of guilt passing through her eyes, although that hadn't been his intent.

"I'm not sorry, by the way," he told her. "I'm not sorry about anything that's happened these last few days." In fact, he couldn't deny the sudden and niggling feeling that perhaps he'd somehow gotten in too deep here. *So maybe I'm* worried—*but not sorry.*

"I'm glad," she said, gazing lovingly into his eyes. And he wanted not to see that look, but it was there, reminding him once more how much this mattered to her. And how much it could matter to him if he let it. But he *couldn't* let it.

"So while we're on the subject of me," he joked, more than ready to put things back where he liked them—into that easy, fun place, "I need help getting another area of my life in order."

"Don't tell me there's more to your saga?" she asked with a giggle.

"Afraid so." He attempted to look very grave. "All the walls and shelves in my condo are empty. Can you help?"

She took on a playful yet prim expression. "Well, I do consider myself a young Martha Stewart."

"I was thinking," he said, although the idea had just popped into his head, "that maybe I could talk you into helping me decorate my condo. After work tomorrow? I want the place to start looking like someone actually lives there, but I'm not really an interior decorating sort of guy." And considering all the thoughts about ending this racing through his head, the idea sounded positively ludicrous, but there it was, out there between them—and he was dying for her to say yes.

"I'd love to," she said.

He smiled, already looking forward to it. "And I'd offer to make dinner for you when we're done—but I only have beer and butter in my refrigerator."

She smiled back. "Clearly, decorating isn't your only homemaking deficiency. Although this explains why you think grilled cheese and Doritos qualify as a meal. Why don't we hit the grocery store, too?"

"You wouldn't mind doing that with me?"

"Not at all. And I'd hate to picture what you'd whip up using beer and butter."

"That would be great," he said. "I mean, I don't even know where the grocery store *is* yet."

So now they'd made their next plans, they knew when they'd be together again, and for Ryan, that usually meant it was a good time to call it a night. But it was so damn cozy cuddling with her on the couch, and he knew from recent experience it was even better snuggling naked with her beneath the sheets. Add her sweet eyes into the mix and she was making it hard to leave.

"So," he said, leaning to place a tiny kiss on the tip of her nose, "feel free to kick me out if you'd rather be on your own—but would you care if I, uh, stayed the night?"

She shook her head lightly, spoke softly. "No, Ryan. I'd like that." No hesitation. Which he loved. But also hated—for conflicting reasons.

He'd suspected she would, of course, and he wished he'd done it only to please her—but he hadn't. Staying over, letting it be that kind of thing, was the one mistake he'd *not* made with her so far—until now. Yep, now the mistake list was complete.

Yet knowing he would hold her all night and wake up to her smile in the morning made it worth it.

———

FRIDAY WAS USUALLY a busy day at the Two Sisters Pub—weekend events at the Convention Center often started on Friday, and more people ate out at week's end in general. Still not having heard from Martin, Penny placed one last phone call to him that morning before things got hurried, and she listened to that irritating message one final time. But tomorrow he would be home—unless he was lying dead in a ditch somewhere, which she doubted—and then phone calls wouldn't matter anymore. She wondered if this horrible waiting was karmic punishment for what she'd done while he was away.

After that, though, there was little time to think about Martin, and not even much room for Ryan in her mind once the lunch rush began. Still, knowing she would see him in a couple of hours gave her an extra burst of energy. She was looking forward to their excursion tonight. Something about helping a man shop for groceries and organize his home seemed...personal. And they'd already gotten more than a little personal, of course, but to Penny, this felt like an invitation into his life. She still had no idea how things would shake out once Martin returned, but tonight's get-together had given her hope where before there had been none, or at least only a little.

She felt bad leaving Patti, considering the lunch crowd still hadn't waned at one thirty—a large trade convention was in town. But Patti assured her she had it under control and would call in an extra bartender for the evening if business warranted. Penny had told her sister what she and Ryan were doing tonight, and Patti had acted as if they were going to pick out china patterns together. "Oh, Pen, I'm so happy for you," she'd said, giving her a hug.

Ryan showed up at her house at two o'clock as scheduled, and just like every time she saw him, her heart trembled. He kissed her hello, held her close, and smiled down into her eyes. "So," she said, twining her arms around his neck, "is that a mouse in your pocket, or are you just glad to see me?"

Confusion shadowed his eyes. "A mouse?"

"A computer mouse," she said with a laugh. "I'm trying to...speak your language, follow a common theme."

"Ah." He tipped his head back in understanding, then

laughed, too. "That's very funny, but, uh…couldn't you have picked something a little bigger?"

Grinning up at him, she tilted her head in thought. "Okay, is that a…hard drive in your pocket?"

He grinned. "Now that's more like it—and yes, I'm *very* glad to see you."

They'd both agreed that to start working in his office at this point would still be a bad idea. Now that they had a hard copy of her notes, it might've been more convenient, but Penny worried about Martin's other employees seeing them together. She feared if they spent time in the rest of the staff's presence, they might slip up—get caught making eyes at each other or accidentally say, "See you tonight," upon parting ways.

As things were, they already knew they worked well enough at her house, so after sharing another kiss or two, they took their respective places at her desk and got down to the business of designing the food and drink portion of the system.

Three hours later, they'd covered a lot of ground, yet had barely made a dent in the pub's menu. "See," he said, "I told you this would be the long part."

Yet she didn't mind. She loved their daily work date, and she wouldn't complain if they never finished.

"But it's enough for today," he told her, "and besides, we've got a big night of groceries and decorating ahead of us. Still up for it?"

She nodded. "Of course."

"Then I guess I should head down to the office. The sooner I go, the sooner I can meet you at the condo." With that, he pressed his spare key into her hand and she closed her fist around it. He'd explained earlier that one of Martin's clients had called this morning requesting a short meeting late today, so Ryan had promised to see the guy.

He'd offered to come back and pick up Penny afterward, but she'd suggested that she drive to his place on her own while he was busy, to start checking out the space and thinking about decorating possibilities.

"1201 in Adam's Landing," he reminded her.

She nodded. It was one of the poshest developments on the river.

"And, uh, try not to be intimidated by all the boxes sitting around."

"Maybe I'll start unpacking some," she said, then caught herself, wondering if that was too personal an offer to make. "I mean, if you don't mind. If you'd rather I didn't—"

He shook his head. "I don't mind at all. I'd be grateful, in fact."

"You're sure you don't mind me snooping through your things?"

"I've got nothing to hide. No velvet handcuffs or anything like that," he added with a wink.

She playfully punched him in the arm, then kissed him goodbye, all the while thinking that despite her initial mortification, sharing heart-shaped handcuffs with Ryan had turned out to be an amazing experience.

———

"WHAT A FABULOUS PLACE," she told Ryan when he arrived at his condo ninety minutes later. She stood looking out the plate glass window that covered the front wall of the living room, the view of the river and the bridges that crossed it almost as breathtaking as the one at the park.

"Thanks." He stepped up beside her for a moment, then turned to toss his suit jacket over the back of a leather recliner before loosening his tie. "It's pricy, but I like it.

Which reminds me, did you get any great decorating ideas?"

"Well, I'll want to find out what color schemes you like. And I know a few shops with lots of décor and accessories that would fit great here. After we go through your boxes and get things into place, maybe we can plan a small shopping excursion."

"Sounds good."

"By the way, I started unpacking your dishes into the cabinets. If you don't like where I put things, we can rearrange them."

He smiled. "I'm sure I'll love it. I was avoiding that job because I couldn't decide where everything should go."

"Oh, and your answering machine is blinking."

Ryan spun toward it, then pressed the playback button. "Hey, Ryan, it's your big brother. Just called to see how the new job is going. Mom said you liked it but that you're not eating right." The brother laughed good-naturedly. "Give me a call sometime."

Ryan raised his eyebrows. "That's surprising. I hardly ever hear from Dan."

Despite the things he'd told her about his family, she suspected he had his mom and dad pegged all wrong. "Will Dan or your parents come visit? See your condo?"

He shook his head. "I doubt it. Dan and I aren't close, and Mom and Dad are basically homebodies, not into long car trip or big cities. And they'd probably find this place a little extravagant. They like simpler things."

"So do I," she reminded him. "But this place is wonderful."

"Still, my parents and I are worlds apart. They're in the old world and I'm in the new. They have very old-fashioned values."

155

She flinched at the words—then suffered surprise at her own reaction.

"What's wrong?"

She sighed. "Well, until a few weeks ago I guess I thought of *myself* as someone with old-fashioned values. But now…"

He gave her a scolding smile, then pulled her down onto the dark, leather sofa. "It's okay to be versatile, Penny. It's okay to have your own ideas and feelings about things."

"But when I imagine the looks on my parents' faces if they could see what we've been…"

He let his eyes go wide. "Oh my God, woman. You're not *supposed* to imagine that—no one is. Don't go there. As long as the things you do feel right to *you*, then that's right enough."

Penny considered what he'd said. She wasn't sure how she'd ended up on this ride where one minute she was announcing how wild she was and the next, recanting and worrying about it; she supposed it was just a difficult transition for the ultimate good girl to make. Yet Ryan was going through it with her. He had started exploring it with her just like she'd fantasized about, and now, bit by bit, he was helping her get the emotional parts of it in place, too.

"Maybe you'd do well to remember those words yourself, Mr. Pierce," she said, thinking of all he'd shared with her last night, the window he'd opened into his past, and even his present.

He gave her a knowing smile. "Okay, are we talking about my parents, or are we talking about me, you and Martin?"

"I don't know—maybe all of it. Maybe we should *all* just be a little more trusting of our feelings sometimes."

"And not worry about who gets hurt or what anyone thinks of us?"

"I didn't say *that*. But I think there must be a happy medium, and the trick in life is finding it."

Ryan simply nodded, but where he and Penny were concerned, he didn't know how they were going to reach any such ideal medium. He understood how what she was saying applied to his relationship with his parents—that if he liked his life and knew he'd done his best, that should be enough. And he also understood how it applied to her recent self-discoveries—if she liked herself, that was all that mattered. But when Martin entered the picture, things weren't nearly so cut and dried. No matter how he looked at it, one thing here never changed: He needed this job and he wasn't sure he'd get another opportunity this good if he messed this one up.

"Well," he said, having had enough of this inner contemplation, "as soon as I change clothes, we can venture out to the store."

"I checked out your fridge and pantry," she told him as he got to his feet. "You've got a lot of room, so we can stock up and you shouldn't have to do this again for months other than a few basics."

He grinned down at her. "I've said it before and I'll say it again—a woman after my own heart."

Though as he made his way to the bedroom, he couldn't deny that the revelation was starting to trouble him, more and more. After waking up to her pretty eyes and tousled hair this morning, he'd thought about her as he'd driven home to shower, then all day at the office, too. He'd even found himself popping into the lobby for no good reason around lunchtime, hoping to catch her daily sandwich delivery, but he'd missed it.

And the sex. Every single time it blew his mind. He never got used to the way it felt to be inside her, the way his soul ached when she moaned for him. Even just kissing her made him feel like a lovesick teenager.

He slid a burgundy golf shirt over his head. *So much for settling down in Cincinnati.*

But then, if not for the wild parts, and if not for the risk factors, he supposed this *could* feel settled. Once they got past the sexual frustration, everything with her had come so easy—relaxing in the park together, eating together, talking in bed, even telling her about his parents and brother, and about losing his job at ComData. And every time they were apart, he found himself looking forward to the moment they'd see each other again.

And now they were going grocery shopping. It sounded ridiculously domestic. And he was still looking forward to it.

Throwing on a pair of blue jeans, he sighed, ran a hand back through his hair, then took a glanced in the mirror. *You'd better get control of this situation. Soon. Before it all blows up in your face.*

———

THE CART RYAN pushed overflowed with everything from milk and eggs to a variety of frozen foods. "Hey, look—goetta," Penny said, pointing to the sign on one of the refrigerated bins. "Want some?"

"*Goetta?* What is it?"

"Oh," Penny said, "I guess it's one of those regional foods. It's…um, kind of a sausagy, oatmealy sort of thing."

He laughed. "No thanks." She'd been a huge help to him so far and made this task much more fun than it would have been otherwise, but every now and then she tried to get him to buy something that just wasn't on his personal menu.

She turned to face him from the other end of the stopped cart. "Are you sure? You can do a lot of good stuff with goetta."

"No goetta," he said with a decisive point of his finger. "I mean it. I just don't think I'm a goetta guy." Prior to this, he'd also had to convince her he wasn't a ricecake or hummus guy.

Before she could protest further, he backed the cart away from her, then swung it down the next aisle. Glass-fronted freezers filled with ice cream spanned its length. "Now, this is more like it," he murmured, studying his choices, then grabbing tubs of French vanilla, cookies-and-cream, and double chocolate.

Penny leaned around to pat his stomach. "I can't believe you maintain this with these kinds of shopping habits."

"I won't be back for months, remember? This is a stock-up trip."

"Ooooh," she said then, stepping past him, her focus having shifted to something behind him. "Hot fudge."

When he turned to find her examining a rack of ice cream condiments, he witnessed a familiar and all too alluring look in her eyes before she caught him watching, then lowered her gaze. Considering how well he was beginning to know her in certain ways, he understood exactly what that look meant. He arched one eyebrow and grinned.

"What?" she asked.

But those innocent eyes weren't working on him this time. "You've got a hot fudge fantasy. Don't deny it."

She gasped. "I…" She shook her head helplessly. "How did you…?" Then she gave it all up. "Oh, darn it, all right, I do. So sue me."

He smiled in triumph. "And you can't even blame this one on Patti."

Her blue eyes went wide. "She *did* buy me those things —I swear it."

He laughed, realizing he loved teasing her way too much, then stepped up close to her in the aisle, which was desolate except for them. "You should quit being so defensive. It just so happens that…"

"What?"

She peered up at him as he cast his most suggestive grin. "I have a hot fudge fantasy, too." Or at least he did now.

And he enjoyed seeing the shock on her face melt into something a little more lurid as he tossed two jars of microwavable hot fudge into the cart.

She glanced down at where they lay atop a bunch of canned goods. "Uh, isn't that kind of a lot?"

He shrugged. "For you, me, and three tubs of ice cream? I don't think so."

———

BACK AT RYAN'S, they filled his refrigerator and pantry with groceries, then Penny showed him how she'd arranged his cabinets. After unloading some glasses, pots and pans, and a few dishtowels and potholders, the kitchen felt livable. "See how fast that went with your guidance?" he said. Then he placed his hand on the back of her neck and pulled her in for a kiss. "Thank you for helping me."

After that, they worked in the living room. When she'd arrived, only basic furniture and the big screen TV had been in place, and a pile of boxes had rested in one corner. Within half an hour, lamps dotted the room, pillows and a throw made the couch cozier, and she'd located a decorative plate that added some character to the coffee table. Next, she put Ryan to work hooking up his DVD player and other electronics while she started filling built-in shelves with books and bric-a-brac, including a couple of framed photos she'd unpacked.

One of the them captured four guys with backpacks and sleeping bags standing in front of an SUV. When she held it up, Ryan explained that he and his college buddies always got together for a hiking trip every fall. They were scattered across the country now, but they considered the hiking trip sacred.

The other picture was a family photo, although she didn't call this one to his attention. In it, the Pierces and their two grown boys stood next to a Christmas tree, the father spreading his arms around each of his sons. They looked like nice people, although she had to admit Ryan was right—he stood out in the crowd. He was taller and broader than his father or brother, and more stylishly dressed. And when she looked at the photo, somehow her heart nearly broke into pieces with the simple yearning to be with him. How could he not realize what an amazing man he was? She turned to watch him fiddling with wires and cables on the floor not far away and thought about his stinging belief that his parents didn't care much about him. And she almost said *I love you*—because she really thought it might be true, more and more all the time now, and she wanted him to know.

Thank God she realized it was the move of a lunatic before she actually did it.

"What's up?" he asked, catching her look.

"Just wondering how it's coming over there."

He laughed. "I know it seems like a mess right now, but five minutes and I'll have it all up and running."

"What's next?" she asked, done with the shelves.

"You wanna order a pizza or something? I don't know the good pizza places around here yet."

"One LaRosa's pizza, coming up." She tossed her empty boxes in a pile next to the wall-spanning window en route to the phone, but the view stopped her progress. Outside, darkness hovered and the sunset glowed magnificently over the river. Streaks of electric pink blazed across the horizon to the west, and tiny dots of light sprinkled the hills on the opposite bank that led down to the Ohio. "Oh, Ryan, come look at this. Is it like this every night from up here?"

He joined her, sliding his arms around her waist from behind. "I don't really know. I'm usually working or having fun with *you* this time of night," he said, sounding playful. "But it's pretty great, isn't it?" He leaned forward, dropping one delicate kiss on her neck as they took in the spectacular colors, streaks of plum now twining their way through the pink splash of sky.

"So what do you wanna do after we eat pizza?" she whispered up to him.

"Easy," he growled. "Break into the hot fudge and have you for dessert."

———

"WE'RE A MESS," Penny sighed as she kissed him.

"I know." He leaned in to lick the remnants of chocolate that had somehow ended up on her cheek.

"I'm exhausted." She reached to kiss him once more.

"You wore me out, too."

They lay in Ryan's bed on sheets he'd promised were old, and thank goodness, because they'd never be the same again. And Penny didn't think hot fudge would ever *taste* quite the same again, either.

"I should shower," she suggested.

"Afraid you'll have to wash your hair while you're at it." He ran his fingers down a long lock now caked with partially dried fudge.

Suddenly amused almost beyond her comprehension, Penny rolled over on her back and started laughing.

He smiled down on her in the lamplight. "What?"

"I can't believe we just did that." It had been so freeing, so sensual, and so…incredibly easy.

"Oh, come on," he teased. "Considering some of the other stuff we've done over the past week, what's a little hot fudge?"

She smiled up at him, then used her thumbnail to chip away a tiny blot of dry chocolate from his chin. "It was fun, wasn't it?"

"The hot fudge? Or everything else, too?"

"The hot fudge," she said. The warm sensation of having it dribbled over her and then watching him lick it off had been nothing less than exquisite. "But everything else, too."

"Starting a week ago tonight," he said, and she shook her head in disbelief. She couldn't believe they'd gotten together only a week ago! But then again, given *how* they'd gotten together, maybe what'd followed had been somehow inevitable, meant to be. "It's been one hell of a week," he added, nuzzling her ear, then softly biting her neck.

"I was just thinking the same thing."

I was just thinking, in fact, that I love you.

It had struck her in an undeniable way during their incredible sexual connection just now and, suddenly, not a shred of doubt remained. When she'd heard his deep moan and felt his body collapsing against her, she'd realized how profoundly she cherished bringing him pleasure and she'd known—beyond question, with no doubt—that it was indeed love.

She couldn't tell him, of course, since nothing had really changed between them except for the utter certainty in her heart. But it was real and solid and surrounded her like a warm cocoon from which she could never escape, could never *want* to escape.

She wasn't afraid anymore, or nervous about anything they did together. She had moaned and laughed and relished every moment of living out her hot fudge fantasy with Ryan. Not one scrap of inhibition or "good-girlness" had snuck in. She'd simply been having decadent fun with the man she loved—nothing more, nothing less. It was as if the fresh and sure revelation that this was definitely love had cleared her head in other ways, too, freeing her from the chains she'd shackled herself in somewhere along the way.

And maybe that had happened quickly, but wasn't it like that sometimes? Love at first sight? Who didn't know a couple—or more than one—who had met and fallen for each other instantly? Though they hadn't known each other long, it felt to her as if they had, as if all this had been growing in her from the moment they'd met. And now it was blooming inside her, like a spring flower in the sun.

A few minutes later, she watched as Ryan dragged himself up from the chocolate-stained sheets to make his way to the shower, both of them laughing again at what a mess they were. He soon returned from the bathroom with a plush towel hooked at his waist. "Shower's free if you're recovered enough," he said with a wink.

"I'm getting there." She sighed happily.

He flashed a grin. "While you're getting cleaned up, I'll get these sheets off the bed and into the washing machine before I end up tracking chocolate footprints through the condo."

Soon after, they found themselves both wrapped in towels and snuggling on his couch, laughing still more because he hadn't had any luck locating clean sheets. She wanted to spend all night in his arms, and she hardly cared if it was in a bed or on the couch or on the floor.

"I guess Martin never returned your calls or you'd have mentioned it," he said as she settled into his arms.

"No, he didn't, and I don't understand why. But I suppose it doesn't matter much now."

"Why not?"

"He'll be home tomorrow," she said. "So maybe I was meant to tell him face to face."

As his body tensed beneath her, she gazed down on him in the darkened room, lit only by the glow from the city below gleaming through the large window. She couldn't make out his expression, but she sensed his surprise at the reminder and it tightened her chest. Their happy mood had just shifted into something else.

Just then, the phone rang across the room. Ryan made no move to get it, so they both lay silently listening as the answering machine picked up. "Hello, Ryan, it's your mother. I'm calling with some good news about Dan. I ran into Ellen Winston at the beauty parlor and she let out a secret—the alumni association at the high school is planning to give your brother a lifetime achievement award this fall! He'll be the youngest recipient in the school's history! Be sure not to breathe a word, though, since it'll be a surprise at the alumni banquet. Call me and I'll fill you in on the details. Bye."

The phone went quiet then, the answering machine clicking off.

Penny heard Ryan's sigh beneath her and they started talking at the same time.

"Ryan, they—"

"I hate to—"

They both stopped.

"You first," she said.

He took a deep breath and the room seemed too quiet. She waited, but he didn't reply, although his heartbeat sped up beneath her palm.

"What is it?" she whispered.

"I was just thinking," he began, "that maybe we should, uh…take a little break from each other."

A enormous knot formed in Penny's stomach, and another in her throat.

"Since Martin's coming back tomorrow," he went on. "Just until you get a chance to talk to him and we see how it goes. You know?"

Her breath felt shaky and she inhaled, then exhaled, in order to try smoothing it out. *This is a fling. Just a fling. At least that's what it is to him. And you knew that. And you were okay with it. Or so you claimed. So you have to be okay with it now.* She had to deal with it like an adult. She had to forget the love pounding in her chest and seeping through her pores.

"Yeah," she finally said around the lump that made talking difficult. "That would probably make sense." And as much as she hated it, it *did* make sense. Because Martin could easily show up at her place, or see them out somewhere together, and neither of them wanted to be "caught" together, albeit for different reasons. It had been easy to push aside thoughts of Martin while he was away, but she didn't want to hurt him. And she needed time to deal with the whole stupid proposal issue. So it made *perfect* sense.

Only it broke her heart at the same time. Because who

really knew what "a little break" really meant or what would happen between them now? And the fact was, as long as Ryan worked for Martin, their relationship would probably be a problem—and seeing Grace in the park the other day had made it clear to her that she didn't want to feel like they were sneaking around, even if they weren't doing anything wrong. Ryan might call it "a little break," but no matter how she sliced it, in the big picture, this was probably just him trying to let her down easy.

So much for loving him. And so much for an invitation into his life. Instead, the night had turned into an invitation *out* of it.

Chapter Nine

Ryan had known Martin was due back at some point, of course, but he hadn't quite figured out that it was *now*. Maybe he'd just been in denial, because God knew it was easier to just not think about his return. But Penny's words —"He'll be home tomorrow"—had been like a cold glass of water splashing him in the face. A wake-up call. A huge sign that read Think About Your Future bashing him over the head. The timing of his mother's phone message hadn't helped, either.

"And I have plenty to stay busy with," he went on, anxious to fill the sudden void between them. Funny how shared silence could be so nice one minute, yet so awkward the next. "Like I told you, the food order part of the system will be the most time consuming, even more so on my end. So let's plan on, uh, not getting together in the afternoons until you hear from me, okay?"

"Okay," she said. But her voice came out far too soft, making his heart clench.

This was it, that moment he'd dreaded, the moment where he hurt her.

And he sure as hell hadn't planned on it happening tonight, and he wished he could do something to stop it, change it. But finding out Martin would really be back tomorrow, back in her life and back in his, meant the fantasies were over, at least for a while.

He didn't know what else to say and wished he'd been better prepared, wished he'd realized this was coming so suddenly. Her body had gone rigid in his arms, and he gently stroked her soft shoulders, hoping somehow to soothe her, to let her know this wasn't how he really wanted things.

Then he realized he could just say that. Maybe it would help. It was something anyway. "This isn't what I want, Penny. You know that, don't you? You know I wish things were different."

"Of course."

He felt how tough and agreeable she was trying to be, but he heard the underlying sadness in her voice just the same.

He squeezed her tight, wanting to let her know he cared and hoping she could feel how hard this was for him, too, then he dropped a short kiss on her forehead.

That was when she pulled away. She was off the couch, free of his embrace, before he knew what had hit him.

"Penny, where are—" Lamplight suddenly blinded him and he held a hand up to shield his eyes, squinting at her as she moved through the living room. She held her towel closed tight as she stooped to snatch up the clothes she'd shed earlier before even making it to his bed.

"I'm gonna head home," she said without looking at him, obviously struggling to sound casual as she slid her panties on without dropping the towel.

"Penny"—he rose on one elbow to look at her—"you don't have to go."

Letting the towel fall to her feet, she kept her back to him as she hooked her bra and slid the straps onto her shoulders.

"I know," she said, shifting slightly toward him as she reached for her shorts. She was forcing a smile, trying her best to look pleasant—and he still wasn't buying. "But I'm tired and it's late and...well, maybe it's best, all things considered."

He sighed and got to his feet, fastening his towel at his waist as he neared her.

She pulled her T-shirt on over her head.

Stopping in front of her, he ran a hand back through his hair and felt like the ass of the century. "I really know how to ruin a nice evening, don't I?"

"You didn't ruin it." She shook her head insistently. "And I understand. You're right about this." Rising up on her tiptoes, she kissed his cheek, then moved past him toward the door, grabbing up her purse on the way.

And he followed, thinking he should do something, not let her leave this way—but no words of protest ever left his mouth, and within seconds, she was disappearing out his door and up the hall toward the elevator.

He stood in the doorway watching after her, realizing he hadn't even said goodbye. Emptiness washed through him when he heard the elevator ding around the corner, knowing he'd let her leave without doing a damn thing to prevent it.

But he'd known it would come to this. He'd known it would have to. And surely she had, as well. Hadn't she?

Shaking his head in regret, he stepped back inside and shut the door. This would all be okay in the end. It would have to be, because he'd had no other choice. And it wasn't like he'd told her he didn't want to be with her or thrown her out on the street. He'd simply made a move that seemed sensible for them both.

And as for what this weekend would be like without her, well, it would be like all the *other* weekends he'd ever spent without her—no big deal. He was a self-reliant guy, the type who didn't mind moving to a strange city without any friends, who liked people but didn't tend to get deeply attached.

Basically, it would just be…getting back to normal.

But since when did normal sound so damn lonely?

————

RYAN SPENT most of Saturday at Schuster Systems, working on the Two Sisters project. He no longer used Martin's office, not just because his own computer had arrived, but because Martin was his boss, the corner office belonged to him, and Ryan wanted to make damn sure he remembered that. Squeezing himself into his matchbox-size office seemed a good way to get it through his head once and for all.

If you wanted to go places in a company, you started at the bottom and paid your dues. And you followed the rules, both the written and unwritten ones. Unwritten ones included: *Don't have sex with the woman the boss wants to marry* and *Don't keep doing it over and over.* He was going to start paying attention to the pecking order here, staying in his place and keeping his nose to the grindstone, being that "good boy" he'd once told Penny he'd come here to be.

He sank into the work for long stretches and let it remind him how much he loved what he did. He was a damn good programmer and designer and it always showed in the finished product. It also temporarily got his mind off of *her.*

Of course, all that changed every time he stopped to go to the bathroom or get something to drink from the kitchen, like now. He stood before a snack machine perusing candy bars and, of course, they were all made of chocolate—one of the many things that automatically turned his mind to Penny. Limousines, bathtubs, candles, bras. *Feet*, for God's sake! And now chocolate. Finally deciding the thought of chocolate without her underneath it sounded unbearable, he chose peanut butter crackers instead.

Snatching up the package from the machine's bin, then grabbing a soft drink, he made his way back toward his office. Damn, that'd been bad timing last night. He rolled his eyes, remembering what he'd done. *Nice, Ryan, real nice.* Slather the girl in hot fudge, have wild sex with her like there's no tomorrow, then toss her out of your life. He didn't think he'd ever done anything so cold. Although it hadn't seemed that way at the time. When it had been happening, he'd kept thinking *sensible, sensible, sensible*—but today, it just seemed *cold*.

This is all Martin's fault. He wanted to believe that as he caught sight of the man's name on the office door down the hall. But it wasn't true. The fault here lay with nobody but himself. For needing Schuster Systems so badly. For screwing up all his other chances. The blame was on him.

It would serve him right if she forgot all about turning down Martin's proposal and married him anyway. Of course, she'd said there was nothing real between them, but what if she'd exaggerated, merely been swept up in passion? What if there *was* a real romance there, a real connection? And what if it appeared a hell of a lot better to her right now than Ryan did? After all, look at all Martin could offer her. Stability, in multiple ways. Financial security *and* a lasting commitment.

Ryan let out a cynical laugh as he settled behind his desk. Ironic that stability was the one thing *he* craved—he wanted a job that would last, a life that felt comfortable and dependable—yet it remained the one thing he couldn't even begin to offer Penny.

Nonetheless, the idea gave him pause, halting him in mid-keystroke. Was that what he wanted? To offer her stability?

The very notion gave him that familiar sense of completeness he got from her, for the first time since she'd walked out his door last night. He'd thought he was taking control of the situation by putting distance between them, but suddenly he feared he'd let it get even further out of his grasp. At least when they'd been together, he'd known *that* part of his life was good and secure.

Secure. Stable. The very things he wanted, he found…with her.

He took a deep breath, then let it back out, realizing he'd never felt quite so secure in his life as he had with Penny. She was always so honest, so sweet, so affectionate. He'd never had to worry that she'd suddenly leave him, because she always wanted him to stay. He'd never had to fear that she wanted him to change—wanted *anything* to change—because he'd seen in her eyes and felt in her touch that she liked him just as he was. She didn't care about his past, or even if he had a questionable future. She just liked him. *More* than liked him. He knew that. Had seen that and couldn't deny it. She cared for him…and, damn it, he cared for her, too.

He…*loved* her.

What else could make his heart hurt so bad right now? What else could fill him up so much whenever she was around? What else could have him risking his career over a touch, a kiss, an embrace?

It was true. *He was in love with Penny Halloran.*
And he'd pretty much thrown her out of his life.

———

PENNY HAD WAITED all day on Saturday to hear from
Martin. When afternoon had ebbed into evening, she'd
called him on his home line...and gotten yet another
recorded message. "You've reached Martin Schuster.
I'm not available to take your call, but if you leave
your name and number, I'll get back to you. Or you
can try reaching my office during business hours at..."
and he gave the number. She'd hung up in total frustration. What on earth was going on here? Where
was he?

Now it was Sunday afternoon and she was nearly out
of her head. Could something actually be wrong? Could
he *really* be lying in a ditch somewhere? After all, no one
had heard from the man or officially account for his where-
abouts for a week now.

"Let's go shopping," Patti said, standing in Penny's
foyer.

"Shopping?" She'd just filled her sister in on the latest
turn of events, including the facts that she still hadn't
talked to Martin and that her love life was in shambles.
"I'm hardly in the mood for shopping."

"Oh, come on. A little retail therapy always does a girl
good. We'll buy you something new to wear, something
sexy, something to reflect the new you."

But Penny only sighed. "I'm not in the mood to be
sexy, either. After all, at the moment, I have no one to be
sexy *with*."

Her sister raked a dismissing hand down through the
air. "Details, details." She grabbed Penny's wrist in one

hand and scooped up Penny's purse in the other. "Come on. I'll drive."

After she let Patti drag her from the house, she stopped and dug in her purse for her keys. As she locked the door, though, she glanced down to see Ryan's spare condo key still hanging from the ring. It only added to her depression.

"I could kill that guy for putting you through this," her sister said, apparently realizing just how deep Penny's despair ran.

"*Which* guy?" She was thinking about Ryan, of course, but she had a feeling Patti meant…

"Martin," Patti confirmed.

Yet Penny protested. "He really didn't put me through anything. I put *myself* through it. Considering what I did while he was away, there's no room for anger here."

And all Martin's absence *really* meant was that it would take longer to figure out the real meaning behind Ryan's invitation out of his life longer to find out whether it was permanent. He'd implied it wasn't, but she still questioned whether that was the truth. It had been a long, painful weekend, and now there seemed no end in sight. Her body ached for him, even after just a couple of days.

"This is what I get," she told Patti as they started down the front walk, "for not making sure Martin knew how I felt before moving on. I deserve this."

"No, you deserve Ryan. Although I'm considering kicking *his* butt right now, too."

Penny shook her head as they approached Patti's car. "He's just trying to save his job. You can't blame the guy for that."

"Yes I can. Some things are more important."

"I never asked him for promises," she pointed out, glancing briefly at her sister over the car's roof just before they both ducked inside. "I never asked him for anything more than a good time, fun, sex." She stopped then, turning to gape at her sister in pure horror. "Oh God, I'm a good-time girl! I have indiscriminate sex with strangers! I treat sex like it's nothing!"

Patti tilted her head. "Did it feel like that, Pen? Did it feel like nothing?"

She thought all the way back to the limo, and then to everything after. "Never," she said quietly. And then she admitted one *more* thing to her sister. "I'm in love with him."

"Ah." Patti cast her a consoling glance, after which she started the car and pulled away from the curb. "Well, then, rest assured, you're not a good time girl. Your only crime is falling in love with a guy who isn't ready to give it back."

"And just what am I supposed to do about that?"

Patti shrugged. "Picking up a cute mini-skirt couldn't hurt."

———

ON MONDAY MORNING, Ryan kept his office door wide open, listening. It would happen any minute now. The elevator would ding, the doors would slide open, and Martin's voice would echo through the hallways of Schuster Systems. He would greet Grace, make small talk about his conference, catch up on important messages, then shuffle past Ryan's closet, maybe pausing for a hello. His heart rose to his throat each time he heard the elevator.

When Martin hadn't arrived by nine, Ryan assumed he must be sleeping in. But when the boss still hadn't shown up by ten, he started getting impatient.

He needed Martin to show up. He needed to get his life back to normal. He needed to know Penny had talked to him, needed to somehow find out what she'd said and how it had gone.

Half an hour later, the office remained quiet, everyone busy at work, but still no Martin. Was Ryan the only one to notice his absence? Did everyone else know where Martin was and had just neglected to tell the new guy?

Clicking the Save icon on his computer screen, Ryan made his way to the lobby. Grace looked up from opening the mail when he stopped at her desk. "Yes?"

"Isn't Martin due back today? I haven't seen him."

"He's not back in town yet."

Ryan felt his blood pressure begin to spike. "He's not back? Why not? Do you have any idea?"

Grace flashed the same look one might give a suspected mental ward escapee. "No need to get upset, Ryan. He'll *be* back."

No need to get upset? *No need to get upset?*

But he had to keep his emotions under control. Grace clearly thought he was a psycho. And the fact was, he was starting to *feel* a little crazy upon realizing he'd just spent a weekend apart from Penny—hurting her in the process—for apparently no reason at all.

"I just...need to talk to him about some projects," he said, working to keep his voice even.

"He called to touch base a little while ago."

"What did he say?"

Grace turned her attention back to the mail. "He couldn't talk long, but just told me he'd been delayed. He said he'd call again tomorrow to let me know when he'd be home."

So he hadn't been home this weekend, he still wasn't home now, and might not even be home tomorrow? "What do you think is keeping him?"

As Grace lifted her gaze once more, Ryan wondered if

177

he looked nuts again. "Could be a lot of things. Most likely, some business opportunity came up that couldn't wait."

He nodded, trying tried to act like that was a good enough answer, but no matter what was holding Martin in Vegas, Ryan was starting to think it damned irresponsible of him. He had a company to run. Messages were piling up like crazy. And for God's sake, he'd asked a woman to marry him who was waiting to give him an answer! What kind of a man *was* this?

And to think Ryan had lost his last job for showing up somewhere ninety minutes late.

He returned to his desk and got back to work, but when noon arrived and still his bones ached with missing Penny, he threw down his pencil and pushed to his feet. That was it. He was taking action.

For one thing, he couldn't live with the fact that he'd hurt her.

For another, he was beginning to think he had his priorities screwed up.

Not to mention that he was confused as hell about his recent revelation that he was in love with her.

No wonder he was acting like such a psycho—part of him was still worrying about his job, while another part of him was starting to think ahead out into some impossible, improbable future, and starting to actually *worry* about her wild side. Not that he didn't love it; he adored it! But he'd told her once that they were in different places, and it was true—Penny wanted to explore her sexuality, have fun, lose her inhibitions. And if the job problem wasn't in the way, well, his thoughts might begin to travel in a totally different direction, a direction they'd never travelled before. It had to do with settling down. With one woman. And despite what he thought she felt for him, what if he was wrong and she didn't? Maybe Penny wouldn't even *want* anything long-term.

Aw hell—nothing made sense to him anymore, and this new concern just complicated things further.

"I'm going out for a while," he told Grace as he headed toward the elevator. He had to get out of the office before he lost his mind.

"I already ordered your sandwich. Do you still want it?"

"Yeah, I'll eat when I get back. I just need to run an errand."

Moving through the revolving door onto Walnut Street a minute later, Ryan hit the sidewalk, on a mission. What he planned to do wouldn't even begin to help his confusion or solve their problems, but at least it would let Penny know that she was on his mind, and that he wanted her like crazy.

———

PENNY WENT through the workday in a daze. They were busy for a Monday, and she kept up with the pub's traffic, but she barely remembered what she was doing from one moment to the next. When she left a little before five, she was exhausted, although she knew it was more mental than physical. Martin's unexplained absence was eating at her, and Ryan's *explained* absence was killing her.

Maybe Patti had been right. Maybe her only crime was falling for a guy who couldn't return her feelings no matter how wonderful things seemed when they were together. So she tried not to concentrate on memories of their shared laughter, their sweet quiet moments, their sex, and instead attempted to focus on the fact that none of it had been enough to win his love.

In answer to Patti's relentless prodding, Penny *had* returned home with a new mini-skirt yesterday—not her usual look. She'd also picked up a couple of tops that were more formfitting than the clothes she usually wore. She'd actually enjoyed their spree, and even enjoyed the idea of wearing her new purchases; she was used to wearing flirty stuff *underneath* her clothes, but wearing it on the outside would be a new thing for her—other than the night of the limo encounter, of course. The only problem was, she wasn't sure she'd particularly enjoy wearing her slightly sexy new clothes *for* anyone, *with* anyone, but Ryan.

Swinging the car into the driveway, she dragged herself across the lawn and into the house. As she thumbed through her mail, she noticed her answering machine blinking and absently pressed the playback button—then heard Martin's voice. She dropped the mail on the counter and stared at the phone.

"Penny, it's Martin. Forgive me for not calling sooner—time has gotten away from me here. I wish you were home—I'd hoped we could talk." He paused then, sighing. "As you've guessed by now, I've been delayed, but I'll be back soon and you'll be hearing from me."

When the machine clicked off, Penny just kept staring at it. She was glad he'd finally called, but his vague message about being delayed left her even *more* frustrated. This meant he wouldn't be home tonight, just like he hadn't been home all weekend. And for all she knew, he wouldn't come home for days yet. Something in his voice had sounded so cryptic that it only added to her disappointment. Why hadn't he said when he was coming back? Or what the heck the holdup was?

When the doorbell interrupted her thoughts, she shifted her attention away from Martin to find a delivery man waiting on her front porch. He held a pretty little box covered in tiny red hearts, a red foil ribbon tied in an elaborate bow on top. She'd rarely received a package so lovely, but what on earth…? After signing and accepting it, she shut the door and just gaped at it.

Had Patti sent something to cheer her up? No, they'd spent the whole day together—if her sister had wanted to give her a gift, she'd have done it at the restaurant, or yesterday when they'd shopped together.

And then it hit her. Martin. This was some sort of combination romance/apology/explanation present. He'd said she'd be hearing from him and maybe this was what he'd meant. Sadly, it made the pretty wrapping a little less appealing.

She untied the bow, letting the ribbon drop to the floor, then removed the lid. Nestled in a bed of red tissue paper lay a skimpy, flirty pair of tiger-striped thong panties with a scalloped edge. Oh. My. This was from Martin?

But slowly, warily, another possibility began to nudge its way into her mind just as she reached for the card inside.

For the woman who brings out the animal in me. I miss you.

Ryan

PENNY WENT AS weak as a kitten, even as her heart pounded out of control. She remembered wanting to bring out the animal in Martin, and instead it had happened with someone else—*this* man.

Oh God, she loved him. With all her aching heart.

And she wasn't even sure exactly what the panties

meant, or if they really changed things, but…maybe she could *make* them change.

———

RYAN HAD PLANNED to leave the office by six, head home to change from his suit and unwind a little, and then maybe give Penny a call. Hell, maybe he'd even decide to drive by her house and be so bold to knock on the door, see if she'd gotten his gift, see if she hated him or if maybe the gesture had managed to smooth things over a little.

But when he checked Martin's e-mail right before leaving, he found one that had to be dealt with—which meant so much for leaving by six. A client in California was having system problems and Ryan didn't know anything *about* the guy's system, but he felt obligated to call him back anyway, especially since it was only three o'clock there, and God knew Martin wasn't around to do it.

Two hours later, he hung up the phone. It had taken a while, but he'd figured out the problem and walked the guy through fixing it. After turning off the last light in the office, he made his way up a now empty Fourth Street toward his parking garage. And even if he didn't feel great about much else in his life at the moment, he at least knew he'd put in a good, hard day's work.

The sun was sinking over the river by the time he got home, the Daniel Beard bridge silhouetted in the forefront, reminding him of the sunset he and Penny had shared just a few nights ago. Strange, it seemed more like an eternity.

He wondered if it was too late to go by her place? He knew his little tiger-striped surprise had most certainly been delivered by now, and his skin prickled as he tried to imagine her reaction. He felt like a kid who'd just sent his first love note.

Stepping into the condo, dark but for the pink glow of sky blazing through the huge living room window, he flipped on an overhead light. And he'd been just about to swing his briefcase up onto the kitchen counter when he stopped, his eyes drawn to a piece of paper he hadn't put there. His eyes fell on one simple command, written in red ink.

Come to the bedroom, Tiger.

Chapter Ten

RYAN STOPPED IN THE BEDROOM DOORWAY, STUNNED BY THE sight before him. Penny stood against the open balcony door, arms stretched above her head, wearing nothing but the tiger-striped panties he'd sent her.

The first seductive notes of Al Green's "Let's Stay Together" wafted from the radio by the bed. Her hair spilled over her shoulders in dark blond waves, framing her pretty face and the rounded breasts below, their pink crests beaded. Her hips flared slightly from her narrowed waist, the small swath of tiger print stretching across them. With white sheer curtains fluttering around her in the breeze, she looked like a flesh and bone sex goddess, something he might've dreamed.

But he wasn't dreaming. This was real. *She* was real. He let his briefcase *plunk* to the floor.

"Hello there," she said in a breathy voice that added to his arousal.

"Uh, hi. I see you, uh, got my…"

She gave him a provocative nod. "Do you like?"

"Yeah," he said, adding a deeper, "Oh yeah," as her

hips began to sway in slow rhythm with the music. "Uh, how did you…"

She kept the sexy voice going. "I forgot to return your key."

"I'm glad."

"Me, too," she whispered, but then the sensual look in her eyes softened as her hips stilled. "I missed you, Ryan."

Her words pierced his heart as it beat out of control, and not just with arousal now, but so much more.

He finally left the doorway and went to her. She was so beautiful he almost couldn't bear to touch her, to mar the perfect image before him, to let the moment end. Yet, tentatively, he lifted both hands to her face to give her a slow, lingering kiss. When he pulled back, she looked as awed by his tenderness as he was. His whole body thrummed with emotion—ah, damn it, with love. That quickly she had become so much to him, and his every thought seemed to revolve around her now, like she was the sun to his moon. She was the whole package, his sweet, innocent sandwich girl, his hot, daring sex kitten and everything in between.

He touched her lips with two fingertips. "I've missed your kisses."

Emotion filled her blue eyes just before she threw her arms around his neck, clinging to him. And he savored how much she needed him, knowing now what should've been apparent from the beginning—he needed her just as badly.

When next their lips met, they traded kisses filled with more urgency than he'd ever known, and his hands roamed her tantalizing curves as she worked to get him out of his clothes. Soon he stood naked before her, his arousal brushing her stomach as he drank in the heat that burned in her gaze.

"Lie down," she said.

The demand caught him so off-guard that he merely stared, jaw dropping.

"Remember the night when you did all the work and gave me all the pleasure?"

He managed to nod, letting her back him onto the bed.

"Well," she said in a sultry tone, coming to kneel over him, "I want to return the favor."

He reclined back into the feather pillow, watching as Penny hovered above him, her breasts suspended mere inches from his face as she held him down, pinning his wrists to bed over his head. He was just thinking about lifting his head enough to tug at one nipple, to get one sweet taste of her—when something clicked, twice, and he realized his wrists were encircled with plush fabric.

He knew before he even looked that she'd cuffed him to the wrought iron that lined the top of his bed. A laugh erupted from his throat, yet he quickly let his amusement dissolve into a look of pure lust that he hoped she felt to her core. "Maybe I was wrong," he said. "Maybe *you're* the animal."

"I think we both are—that's why we go together so well." She offered up a suggestive smile. "Although I should warn you, you ain't seen nothin' yet."

With that, she lowered a soft kiss to his lips, then took one last look into his eyes before proceeding downward. She rained kisses onto his neck, his shoulders, his chest, each vibrating through him like the gentle but potent strum of a harp. "You're so sweet," he murmured as her kisses moved lower over his stomach, the muscles in his groin pulling taut.

He let out a soft moan, still watching her every move as his pleasure began to mix with an almost painful anticipation. Was she going to…? He groaned just thinking about…imagining…

And then her soft hand wrapped around his hardness, stroking him lightly. "Ah…" he sighed as her perfect touch pulsed through him.

"I want to make you feel incredible," she said, lifting her eyes to his once more as she lowered a delicate kiss, butterfly soft, to the tip of his arousal. A moan tore from deep in his chest, his entire body tensing with heat and something that felt almost like gratification, except it begged for more.

She took him into her mouth, her warm lips sliding down over him, and he cried out at the shocking depth of pleasure that soaked through his being. His entire world was contained within this bed, within her sweet, hot mouth, within how beautifully sensual she looked doing what she was doing. He recalled thinking once before that it was as if they were the only two people in the world, and it was like that again now. Nothing else existed.

He wanted to touch her, wanted to run his fingers through her hair, feel her silken skin. He wanted to slide her body around and give her the same erotic delights she bestowed on him. More than once, he instinctively reached for her only to be reminded that he was handcuffed to the bed, that she possessed all the control here. He'd felt wholly taken by her in the limo, yet that had been nothing compared to this, the sensation now humming through his chest like lightning in a bottle. Never before had a woman seized all power over him. Never before had he imagined how damn good that could be.

When finally she rose off of him, she gazed down with those innocent eyes that made her such an alluring paradox.

"Ah, honey," he breathed, "I want to kiss you—I want to hold you."

Scrambling up to straddle him, she lowered short, furious kisses to his mouth as she struggled to release his wrists above. When they came free, his arms fell around her waist and he held her tight and whispered how beautiful she was, how completely perfect.

She raised her eyes to his. "Let's go out on the balcony."

His stomach wrenched with the sheer volume of sexual energy she spilled onto him, and he released a low growl in reply. "Did this just hit you, or have you...?"

"Fantasized about it," she finished for him, nodding. "About looking down on the city, feeling like I'm on the top of the world. About the fresh air on my face and the stars up above and the lights at my feet, about feeling like we're out in the middle of all that, yet still it's private, intimate, like no one exists but us."

So she felt it, too, like they were the only two people in the universe. Since the moment he'd seen her tonight, his heart had brimmed so full he feared he might burst apart with the sheer joy she brought him. He adored what she'd done to him, the control she'd exercised over him—but now he needed to show her how *he* felt, needed to fill her with his love. And it was a love he couldn't bring himself to give voice to—not yet—but he hoped he could say it with his body.

She took his hand and led him out onto the small balcony, approaching the waist-high railing. Nothing stood between the high-rise building and the Ohio River but the dark night air—and walls that enclosed both sides of the balcony ensured their privacy. Her hair blew in the breeze as she peered over her shoulder at him, both patient and beckoning. He stood in awe of this glorious, sensual side of her, amazed to be the only man who had experienced it despite knowing it was an innate part of her and that it *had* been long before he'd ever climbed into that limousine.

Stepping up behind her, he brushed her hair aside to kiss her neck, her shoulder, and then he slid his hands around her waist, pressing his erection into the silk of her panties.

"I feel you," she whispered.

As he slid himself against her, she used her bottom to push back. He couldn't see her mouth, but he reached up, grazing his fingertips over her soft lips, then let one finger dip between. Insane, but it felt almost like having that other part of him inside her mouth, and he moaned into her hair, then withdrew his finger and dabbed the moisture onto her nipples, knowing the light summer breeze would torment them even more. She released a sexy sigh, letting her head fall back against his chest, and he gently kneaded her breasts in his hands.

When she turned her head, lifting one arm behind his neck to pull him into a kiss, he slipped his hand into the front of her panties. Her wetness turned him even harder than he already was. She let out a hot gasp of pleasure, moving rhythmically against his fingers while his erection still rubbed her from behind.

Soon the friction was too much and he couldn't wait any longer. "I have to have you," he growled in her ear, using his free hand to peel the panties to her thighs.

"Take me," she breathed.

A soft breeze washed over him as he thrust himself into her sweet warmth. He swore softly and she moaned. Wanting fiercely to connect their bodies in a way they never had been before, he drove himself as deeply inside her as he could. She cried out with each hard stroke, meeting it with the same force. Almost dizzy with pleasure, he reached around her to grab onto the railing as they moved together.

Soon he let one hand slide back down into her moisture, and she responded by easing her body into a more sensuous, grinding rhythm. Moments later, her climax broke, and she called his name in ecstasy. And even admit his excitement, his unadulterated passion, there was something in that—in hearing her say his name that way—that left him feeling...warm, safe. There was something pure in it. Something he'd never felt with any other woman besides Penny.

Still moving inside her, Ryan embraced her from behind and gazed down on the shimmering river below, the headlights winding up Eastern Avenue, the dark, billowing greenery of Sawyer Point—and then leaned near her ear. "We're doing it on the top of the world, honey, just like you wanted."

Even as he continued to thrust into her, her reply came in a heated whisper. "Oh yes."

"You drive me mad," he said, knowing he couldn't keep himself from coming much longer.

And it happened the very second she looked over her shoulder to say, "*You* drive *me*...wild."

———

HE LAY WATCHING her sleep peacefully in his arms, his soul rent with emotion.

After the brain-numbing sex on the balcony, he'd longed to tell her he loved her—and yet he'd held back, confused by everything roiling in his mind. So much remained unresolved. Like where the hell Martin was, for one thing. And how to sort out this mess he'd built around his boss and Penny.

Despite what he'd kept inside, though, their sex had been stupendous, and he wanted more. Easing down in the bed beside her, he dropped a few smooth kisses to her silky stomach until he felt her hand move through his hair and looked up to see her eyes flutter open. Soon he was back inside her, taking them both to heaven again.

Afterward, she laughingly smiled into his eyes, whispering, "I've always wanted to say what I said out on the balcony."

"What's that?"

Again she giggled and looked unaccountably shy. "Take me."

"I liked it," he told her lasciviously, one eyebrow arched.

After a little more flirtatious talk, Penny balanced her chin on his chest and peered earnestly into his eyes. "So… maybe we should discuss things?"

Ryan sighed, then nodded. "I guess we should."

Her expression changed then to something guarded, a little nervous. "I was just wondering what will, uh, happen now? With us, I mean."

"I don't exactly have any firm answers," he confessed, "but the way I figure it, we might as well keep right on seeing each other until Martin finally shows up—because we don't exactly seem capable of stopping anyway."

A pretty blush colored her cheeks as she smiled, but then she turned more serious again. "And when Martin *does* come back?"

He tilted his head. "We play it by ear?"

She nodded, resting her head contentedly against his chest. "A sketchy plan at best," she murmured, "but…"

"A hell of a lot better than being apart," he finished for her.

On that much they clearly seemed to agree.

———

R YAN SAT in his cramped office the next day, staring at the computer screen. He was supposed to be designing the menu system for the Two Sisters Pub project. Instead, he relived the previous night in his head.

But of course, that inevitably—and unfortunately—turned his thoughts to Martin.

Soon realizing his concentration was shot, he left his desk and went to the lobby. He didn't want Grace to think he was a total lunatic over Martin's return, but nearly half the day had passed, and he had to know. "I guess you haven't heard from Martin again," he said, trying to sound very reasonable.

"No, not yet." Grace's voice came as light and airy as usual. "But when I do, I'll tell him how eager you are to speak to him."

Ryan tried not to appear alarmed. "Uh, no need for *that*."

Grace looked doubtful. "Why not?"

"Well, it's nothing that can't wait until he's back. But he didn't give you any idea when he'd return?" He ended with a tilt of his head.

In response, Grace sighed and he got the idea he was getting on her nerves. Understandable, he supposed. "No, he didn't say. But like I told Penny last week, the man has a one-track mind—he's a workaholic. This isn't the first time he's gone away on business, then gotten sidetracked with it."

Ryan just nodded. No matter what the reason, though, the whole thing still made him question the guy's commitment to Penny. Thank God she wasn't marrying him.

"You know what?" he said to Grace, an idea just hitting him. "Don't order my sandwich today. I think I'll grab lunch out." He wanted to leave the office for a while, and he also wanted to see the woman who had turned his heart on end.

When he walked into the Two Sisters Pub minutes later, it bustled with customers. Waiters and waitresses—most of them college-aged—scurried about the room from kitchen to table and back again. Spotting Penny behind the bar serving drinks, he took a stool at one end and just watched her, unnoticed. Simpler Penny had returned again today, her hair falling from the back of a Two Sisters baseball cap, her T-shirt hanging loose over denim shorts. He smiled inside, though, because not only did he love both sides of her equally, he also knew she undoubtedly wore some sinfully pretty bra and pair of panties underneath it all.

"These are for table three, Lisa," she said to a tall blond waitress, shoving a tray of sodas across the pick-up end of the bar. Then an older guy asked for a coffee refill and she reached for the pot with a smile that lit Ryan up inside.

Penny had been floating on air all morning after the night she'd spent with Ryan. She was so in love with him, and she'd been blissfully wild with him, and even though she had no idea what would happen now, nothing had ever felt more right.

"Here you go," she said, filling Mr. Bear's cup. That's how she'd come to think of the man after that first day he'd been in last week. He'd sort of become a regular since then and she'd made sure to treat him with courtesy and speed to make up for her original negligence.

"So," he said, "how'd things turn out with that guy anyway?" When she tilted her head with a confused grin, he added, "The one your sister was teasing you about last week."

Oh, *that* guy. She'd totally forgotten he'd overheard their conversation, but the question drew an easy grin from her. "Things are…coming right along."

Mr. Bear nodded pleasantly and took a sip of his coffee. He'd turned out to be quite nice after all.

"Two Bud Lights and an iced tea, Penny," called Renee, one of the servers, from the pick-up area.

She turned to grab a glass—and spotted Ryan sitting at the end of the bar by the window, watching her. He winked. And that one little wink melted deliciously down through her, instantly bringing back still more amazing memories of last night.

She held up a one-minute finger, then filled the drink order before wiping her hands on a towel and heading down to him. "What are you doing here?" she asked, surprised but happy to see him.

"I'm here for lunch. And because I missed you."

There were moments when she thought her heart would crush beneath the weight of her emotions for him, and this was one of them. "You just saw me a few hours ago, silly," she teased.

"A few hours *too long* ago."

"Penny, I need a bowl of potato soup," Patti called from the other end of the bar.

Darn the timing. She wanted the world to stop, wanted it to be just the two of them again.

"Go on," Ryan told her, clearly seeing her frustration. "I know it's your busy time. I'll just take some of that soup myself whenever you get a chance, and a club sandwich."

"Is that it?"

His eyes turned a little wicked. "Maybe a kiss or two if you can squeeze them in."

"Coming right up." She flashed him a flirtatious smile

before turning to face Patti, suddenly in a total fog when it came to pub business. "Uh, what was it you needed?"

"Soup. Potato soup."

Ryan was right—it *was* her busy time, but she delivered his lunch a few minutes later, and popped back by whenever she had a chance. Even now, when she should be getting used to him, to *them*, the mere sight of him still turned her inside out. And when he leaned over the bar and whispered, "What color is your bra today?" she wanted to forget all the customers, leap across, and attack him.

"That's for me to know and you to find out," she said instead, casting a coy smile. Which was when it occurred to her—she was pretty sure she'd never actually *had* a coy smile before recently. Before Ryan.

By the time he finished eating, the rush had died down, so she was able to spend a little more time talking with him. "By the way," he told her, "your new disc drive and modem were delivered to the office this morning."

She gave a happy sigh. "It'll be nice to have my whole computer back."

"I can install them tomorrow night if you want."

"What's wrong with tonight?"

He grinned. "Well, tonight…I have other plans for you, if you're up for it."

"I'm intrigued, Mr. Pierce. Go on."

"I guess I was thinking," he began on a chuckle, "that maybe we could do all *three* meals together today since we've already accomplished the first two. You wanna make dinner with me at my place? Say around five thirty? I've barely touched any of the food we got at the grocery."

She let a smile unfurl. "Sounds fun."

But that was when he gave his head a decisive shake. "No. Fun," he informed her, "is what we'll have afterward,

195

when I get to see that bra." He concluded with another wink, then rose from his stool and headed for the door.

When he'd gone, she let out an enormous lovestruck sigh. Cooking together sounded nice. Showing him her bra sounded nice. Heck, *everything* with Ryan sounded nice. Still smiling to herself as she anticipated the evening ahead, she reached for a rag to wipe down the bar—and caught sight of Grace watching through the window from the building's lobby.

Oh no—how long had she been standing there? How much had she seen? They hadn't kissed or hugged or anything—but there'd been plenty of giggling and whispering and flirting, and she was pretty sure anyone observing her and Ryan together over the last few minutes would have known they were more than just friends. She felt the blood drain from her face and suspected guilt was written all over it as she and Grace made eye contact. Neither of them waved or smiled. This couldn't be good.

She tensed as Grace walked toward the pub's door. *Please, please, please don't let her know what's going on.* Yet even as she wished it, she knew it was futile.

As Grace approached the bar, Penny braced herself, the ugly feeling of being caught at something ricocheting down through her. She wasn't technically doing anything wrong, but this whole situation sure had a way of making her feel like she was anyway. *I've just lost Ryan's job for him, and somehow unwittingly betrayed Grace, too.*

"Hi," Penny choked out as Grace's green eyes met hers. She tried for a smile but feared it looked forced.

Grace pushed up her glasses. "I came down to tell you Martin just called."

She'd finally heard from him herself yesterday, of course, but for some reason, Penny couldn't have been more stunned if Grace had just said the Queen of England had phoned. "Oh?"

"He's flying back late tonight and will be in the office tomorrow morning. I figured you'd want to know." Grace still didn't smile, but she didn't seem angry or anything, either.

"Of course," Penny said, absently wiping the bar and nodding. "And I'm glad to hear he's coming home. Thanks for letting me know—it was nice of you to come down here just for that."

With a short nod, Grace turned to leave—and Penny's heart began to lighten. Maybe Grace hadn't seen the flirtation between her and Ryan, after all. And she didn't exactly seem as pleasant as usual, but maybe she was just having a bad day or something.

Yet before she reached the door, Grace turned back. "Penny, I don't mean to stick my nose into your business, but…"

Oh no. Here it comes.

"I saw you in the park the other day."

Penny's heart sank like a brick.

"And I saw you just now, too. I don't know the whole story, of course, and I don't have any idea what you plan to tell Martin, but…well, you might at least consider being more discreet."

Penny felt like some kind of cheating wife whose indiscretions had just been plastered across a billboard on I-75. "Grace, I'm…sorry." Her chest hurt and she had no idea what else to say.

To her surprise, however, Grace came back to the bar and touched Penny's hand, damp and clammy now from the rag beneath it. "I'm not the one you should apologize to."

Ugh. Despite herself, tears burned behind Penny's eyes,

threatening to leak free. Because no matter what had changed inside her, she was still a nice person, still a good girl at heart in most ways, and she hated how this looked, and how low it made her feel. She considered telling Grace the truth—at least about her feelings for Martin—but she didn't think it would be right. She couldn't tell Grace she wasn't marrying Martin before telling Martin himself.

As Grace turned to leave again, Penny said, "Grace, wait."

The other woman looked back.

"I can't imagine what you must think of me right now, but it's much more complicated than you know. That's no excuse, I realize, but…well, I think of you as a friend, and I don't want that to change."

Finally, Grace's expression softened. "I think of you that way, too, Penny, and that's why I came in here. I just wanted to remind you that you're not invisible, that your actions may have repercussions."

Even after the door shut behind her, though, Penny still felt like a heel. Grace was right. No telling how many people around the building might know she'd been dating Martin and might have also seen her and Ryan just now, or some other time, like at the park, or the grocery store. The world always got smaller when you were trying to keep a secret.

And now that Martin was *really, finally* coming home tomorrow, and now that so much anticipation and buildup had gathered around his return, she realized just how much she didn't want to hurt him.

Sure, she could try to justify her actions by reminding herself that their relationship had really amounted to nothing more than friendship—but what it came down to was that he'd fallen in love with her and had expected her fidelity for at least as long as it took to mull over his marriage proposal. And okay, yeah, he'd been totally incommunicado, which had made this situation more difficult—but even so, she'd treated him horribly, was *still* treating him horribly. It might not feel like cheating in her heart, but how would Martin see it if he found out?

She truly did care for him. It'd been easy to forget that these past ten wonderful, horrible days, but she did. She'd known him for a long time, having shared two years of friendship before they'd started dating. Although their attempt at romance was recent, their relationship went back further, and she'd just spent a week and a half trampling it without reverence.

Oh sure, she'd told herself she was concerned, she'd let some guilt sift its way into her selfish pleasures—but she'd also conveniently pushed it aside time after time. So even that—her guilt—had been selfish, more about her than about Martin.

But now, maybe for the first time since all of this had started, she really thought about *him*, the man who was her friend, the man who loved her and wanted to build a life with her—and she thought about his real, true feelings, as well. He would be crushed if all this came out. Of course, she still couldn't marry him—but how could she ever really be with Ryan, either, under the circumstances?

And when her thoughts shifted to Ryan, her heart caved in further. Even after all he'd confided in her, about his family, his past job losses, and how important *this* job was to him, she'd still prodded him into bed, over and over. How selfish could she be? And when had she turned into that kind of person?

After all, she'd known from the beginning that this was just about having fun. Sure, they'd had wonderful, wild times together—and sure, they'd been about as intimate as two lovers could be. And he'd even sent her those sexy tiger panties and told her how much he missed her, but…that didn't make it love for him.

He was worldlier than she was in the ways of sex. Well, more worldly than she *usually* was, anyway. Though he'd never said it, she knew instinctively that he'd had a lot of lovers, *casual* lovers. He knew how to flirt—even how to make things amazingly hot and naughty—all without going too deep, and that seemed like the skill of a master of casual relationships. And any secrets he'd ever told her had been only because she'd pushed him with her nosy questions. This was how the world worked—for people other than her, anyway. People could have hot sex, intimate sex, and still feel casually about one another.

So to continue with this relationship, given all that was at stake, had been utterly selfish and thoughtless on her part.

And to keep on with it *now* would be the most selfish act of all, wouldn't it?

For Martin *and* for Ryan.

After all, Martin was coming back. And Grace knew Ryan's secret. How much more dire could things get? And what would happen to Ryan if he lost his job over this, over *her*? She knew now that this was more than just a job to him—it was his way of redeeming himself in his family's eyes, in his *own* eyes. And not only that, but what about the money he sent home to his parents? What if he didn't have it to send anymore? What if one more job loss really *was* the nail in the coffin of his career? All because of her.

As Penny looked down at the same spot on the bar she'd been wiping for several minutes now, she realized a lot rode on this, so much more than her own happiness, so much more than her silly, selfish need to be wild. No matter how she looked at it, she'd spent the last ten days wreaking havoc in the lives of two men she cared for. And if she stopped doing that right now, right this very minute, it might not be too late to make things right again.

———

WHEN SHE GOT HOME at the end of the day, she tried to act like it was any other day. She took off her shoes, looked at her mail, poured herself a glass of iced tea in an attempt to cool herself down. Humidity and scorching temperatures had returned, having edged steadily upward since last week's rain.

But despite her best efforts, it was all just pretend—going through the motions. Because if it were truly just any other day, any average day, she wouldn't hurt so bad inside. Suddenly, her life felt dull, meaningless, empty. Her heart physically hurt in her chest. Funny thing about love. Life had seemed just fine without it—until she'd experienced it, even if only briefly, and then had it taken away.

But no, it wasn't taken away—you're pushing it away. Because you have to.

She'd made a decision, and no matter how many times she went back over it, it seemed like the only right thing to do. As she'd realized during her talk with Grace, Nice Girl Penny really did remain alive and well inside her. Yep, turned out that becoming a sex kitten behind the back of the man who'd proposed to her had nothing to do with her sense of morality. It had just been a lapse in judgment. She'd been lured by the most seductive temptation she'd ever know, but now she had to do that right thing, or she'd never be able to live with herself.

As for Martin, he'd certainly be hurt when she turned down his proposal, but not nearly as hurt as he'd be if he found out the whole truth—that she'd had a full-blown affair while he was away, with his newest employee no less.

And as for Ryan...well, sexual urges aside, he'd get over this quickly. It was simply a matter of putting distance between them, and for more than a day or two this time. Once he refocused on his work, on the reason he'd come to Cincinnati in the first place, he'd forget about her. She'd become nothing more than a pleasant memory, a last, wild fling before he really settled down for good. And then maybe he'd even find someone else, someone who wasn't off limits, someone who wouldn't derail his career, someone who wasn't so reckless and wild that she let nothing else matter but her own pleasure.

Of course, she had to choke back a sob at that last horrifying thought, but then she grabbed the phone and called him before she chickened out. Her stomach churned as she waited for him to answer.

"Hello?" There he was, his beautiful, deep voice echoing across the line and into her heart. How was she going to make herself do this?

"It's, uh, me."

"Hey, where are you?" He sounded happy to hear from her. "I was starting to worry."

She glanced at the clock; it was almost six. "I'm...not coming," she said past the lump in her throat.

Worry invaded his voice. "What's wrong? Car trouble or something?"

"No, but I...uh, spoke with Grace this afternoon. She saw us, Ryan. In the park. And today in the pub. And Martin will be back in the office tomorrow morning."

He stayed quiet for a long, wrenching moment—so she rushed ahead, ready to seal this thing.

"I've thought about it all afternoon, and given the circumstances, I've decided we should stop seeing each other."

More silence resonated through the phone until finally he said, "For now, you mean."

Her chest grew impossibly tight. "No, not just for now. For good," she told him, her heart crumbling. "Your job is important to you, Ryan, for good reason—and I really think you'll lose it one way or another if we stay together. And though I've conveniently avoided I've thinking about it, Martin is a good man, and I've been very unfair to him in all this. If you and I resumed seeing each other, even after I turn down his proposal, I'd still always feel like I'm somehow sneaking around behind his back, committing some crime. He trusted me to be loyal to him while he was away, and I betrayed that trust with you. I can't keep doing it. For both your sakes, this is the right thing to do."

Again, silence lay heavy between them when she finished—and somehow that prodded her to just go on and say everything she needed to, proverbially hammering the very last nails into the coffin of their relationship..

"And it couldn't last forever, right?" She forced a small, surprisingly convincing laugh. "I mean, it was wonderful —*really* wonderful—and I wouldn't trade the time we've spent together for anything. But it was just a fling. And you were probably right all along. We're in different places right now—me wanting to have fun, you wanting to be dedicated to your work—so all in all, it's best to let it end."

She heard his heavy swallow. "Well…what about the, uh, project? Your system?"

"Well, I was thinking maybe Patti could start working with you on it. After all, everything important is in my notes—and to be honest, she's really the administrative brain behind the business, much more than I am. Or… maybe you could talk Martin into shifting the project to someone else for some reason. Either way, I'm confident we can get around that some way."

When he didn't reply to that and silence returned once more, she wasn't sure what else to say. She wanted to get off the phone, end this torture. "Ryan, are you still there?"

"Yeah, I'm here." He sounded tired.

"Thank you," she said on impulse.

"For what?"

"For last week. And last night." She drew in another deep breath. *God, last week. Last night. Intimate perfection. Amazing sex.* Maybe she was crazy to be doing this, but... "Well, I should go now. Bye."

"Penny, I—"

She disconnected the phone with a small gasp, pretending she hadn't heard him say her name. Whatever he had to tell her, she couldn't listen to it. She had to be finished with this or she'd never get through it.

Okay, you did it. Congratulations.

Congratulations on severing the ties on the best thing that ever happened to you.

What now? She felt at loose ends, fidgety.

Her mind raced back to past relationships that had ended, and how a few weeks or months after a break-up, she always reached a time when it felt right to take any of the guy's left-behind things—or even things that strongly reminded her of him—and throw them away. It signified the real end of things for her, the real letting go. A final purging.

Biting her lip in an attempt to crush back her emotions, she decided she should just go ahead and do that with Ryan *now*. After all, they'd been together for a week, two if you counted generously—it had been brief, so why let memories linger on? The sooner she got rid of stuff that made her think of Ryan Pierce, the sooner her heart would be rid of him. A strange thing to try convincing herself she wanted, but she attempted it anyway.

Heading to her bedroom, she opened a drawer and drew out the red handcuffs, then walked to the wastebasket.

Yet just as she was about to drop them inside—she stopped, instead hugging them tightly to her chest. Maybe she *shouldn't* throw them away after all—maybe she was being hasty. Perhaps she should see the heart-shaped cuffs as a keepsake of what they'd shared, a keepsake of the love she'd let go...the love that might have been the love of her life, but she'd done the right thing, for him and for Martin. And that was what life and love was about sometimes, wasn't it? Doing the right thing.

Then she looked down at them, a pair of red, velvet, heart-shaped handcuffs—and started laughing. And before she knew it, she was laughing harder and harder. What a crazy, silly, insane thing to hold on to as a keepsake! What kind of a kinky nutball was she?

She kept on laughing and laughing—couldn't *stop* laughing, in fact—until she realized that somewhere along the way tears had started rolling down her cheeks and that she'd actually started crying instead.

Chapter Eleven

Ryan sat in his office the next morning, watching the
digital clock on his computer screen. 8:07 flicked to 8:08.
He'd come in early in order to beat Grace to the office,
and so far, had avoided seeing her. However, *Martin* should
arrive any minute now. And God only knew what would
happen then. He suspected the rest of the day would be
interesting, to say the least.

It was 8:09 when he thought of Penny. Wow, two whole
minutes had passed without dwelling on her. He remained
as dumbfounded over her call as he had been last night.
He still couldn't believe it. One minute they'd been playfully flirting and planning dinner; the next, she'd not only
stood him up, but given him the boot, too.

He'd wanted to protest, stop her, say the obvious. *If our
time together was so damn special, why are you throwing it away?*
He'd even *started* to say something—but hanging up on him
made her feelings pretty clear. It was hard to believe he'd
misread her so badly, but maybe the woman was even
more complicated than he knew. Maybe she hadn't been as
crazy about him as he'd thought. Maybe, as he'd feared

just yesterday, this was just one big wild affair to her. She'd certainly made it sound like that in the end.

And besides, he couldn't argue with her about the job stuff. He'd been telling himself his priorities were screwed up, convincing himself that maybe the job *wasn't* the most important thing—but what the hell did he think he was gonna do without it? No matter how he stacked it up, the job mattered.

So he hadn't called her back; he'd let it be. He'd let the only woman he'd ever really fallen in love with walk out of his life for a second time in just a few short, agonizing days.

He shook his head, trying to clear it. Talk about a whirlwind relationship—it felt as if a tornado had just swept through his life, leaving little bits of his heart scattered everywhere.

By 8:11, his mind had drifted to the *other* call he'd received last night—which had also left him reeling, in a different way. It hadn't been surprising to answer the phone and hear Dan's voice—after all, he'd never gotten around to returning his brother's call. But the shocking part had been when they'd started talking about Ryan's new job and his condo, and Dan had said, "You've got the life, Ryan. What I wouldn't give..."

"What?" The words simply hadn't computed in Ryan's head.

On the other end of the line, Dan had let out a sigh. "Oh, don't get me wrong. I love Carol, and the kids are great. Life is good. But sometimes I envy you—city life, adventure, something new around every corner. It takes guts to leave behind everything you know and go someplace new—and I just wasn't ever that brave."

Still in a state of heartbreak over Penny, he'd tried to fully absorb his brother's words, make sure he was hearing them correctly. Though they left him stymied.

"I...never felt I had any other choice," he finally explained. "It's what I'd always wanted, just how I saw my life going."

"Well, it still takes courage," Dan said—and then his voice turned uncharacteristically cynical. "Something Mom never stops reminding me."

Okay, wait just a minute here. "What are you talking about?"

His big brother hesitated. "Are you kidding? Mom and Dad never stop singing your praises. *Ryan's doing so well in the city. Ryan's got such a good job. I don't know what we'd do without the money Ryan sends us.* I never hear the end of it."

Ryan sat quietly for a long moment, just breathing into the phone, astonished and speechless—until finally he burst into laughter, not the least of which was due to Dan's imitation of their mother.

"What's so funny, bro?" Dan asked.

"They do the same thing to me, about *you*!"

The brothers had shared a good laugh and a long talk that made Ryan want to get to know Dan better, so much that he'd even invited him to bring his family to Cincinnati for a weekend sometime soon. They'd eventually concluded that their parents must be proud of *both* their sons, just in different ways, and that they simply had the bad habit of touting each son's achievements to the other, instead of doing the opposite. All of which meant, of course, that Penny had been right, despite what he'd so strongly believed. Funny the surprises life could bring you when you least expected them.

At 8:15, the elevator bell dinged, and lo and behold, Martin's voice finally boomed through the office.

"Hello, Grace! I'm back, as promised. Things seem awfully quiet around here—everyone have their noses to the grindstone already? They must be working too hard!"

Ryan flinched, glancing up in the general direction of his boss's voice. Martin sounded a little too…enthusiastic.

"Come to my office and catch me up on anything I need to be caught up on," Martin could be heard saying to Grace then, still sounding overly merry in Ryan's opinion.

Not that he knew the guy well, but the Martin who'd hired him had been much more staid and serious. Pleasant enough, but as Grace had confirmed, Martin was a workaholic and Ryan had seen that in his personality right away.

And this business about them all working too hard. What the hell was *that*?

Then it hit him.

Martin had come home expecting Penny to say yes.

He'd probably wheeled and dealed Schuster Systems into a lot of business at the conference, and now he thought he was on a roll, that things were gonna keep right on going his way. He thought he was getting married.

Unable to bear thinking any further about his boss's misconceptions, he leaned over and nudged his office door shut. The chips would soon fall, and he didn't even know where, but for now he'd just try to get some work done and hope for the best. Although—hell, he didn't even know what the best *was* anymore.

Opening the Two Sisters Pub beta system on his computer, he started inputting more menu information—desserts and variables about each—but his heart wasn't in the work. He continued checking the time without quite knowing why. Maybe thinking of it as a countdown of sorts? For Penny? For Martin? For him?

Soon she'd get to clear her conscience by breaking Martin's heart. And would Grace clear *her* conscience to Martin? Maybe she was doing that right now. Maybe she was telling him exactly what Penny had been up to while he'd been away happily pondering the future he'd hoped to share with her. And when would Penny break the news to him that she didn't want to be his wife? And how would it go? The truth was, he felt bad for the guy—as someone who'd just found out he didn't get to have her in his life anymore, he knew just how badly that hurt.

And that made him wonder what Penny was doing right now, if she was down in the pub yet, if she knew Martin was here—and he even considered calling her to give her a head's up, but had just talked himself out of it when the phone rang.

Could it be her? He grabbed it. "Ryan Pierce."

"Ryan, it's Martin. Can I see you in my office please?" Then he hung up.

Ryan glanced at the clock again. Eight twenty-eight. Plenty long enough that Grace could have told Martin everything. As he pushed back his chair, he heard "Taps" playing in his head. This was it, the countdown was over. He imagined having an actual clock on his desk, with hands, so that he could reach over and stop it like they did in olden times, marking the time of his demise—but you couldn't do that on a computer, damn it. Nope, these days time kept right on moving.

Ryan made his way down the hallway to Martin's office, the place where all this had begun, and his chest constricted as he leaned through the open door. He reached up to loosen his tie, which suddenly seemed to be cutting off his air supply.

"Come in, Ryan," Martin said, glancing up only slightly before returning his attention to the stack of message slips in his hand.

Ryan replied by taking a seat in one of the leather chairs across from his boss's desk. His soon-to-be *ex*-boss, he had a hunch.

"I've got a lot to deal with this morning," Martin said,

lowering the messages to his blotter with a sigh, "but before I do, I want to speak with you."

Ryan nodded and kept eye contact, even as he felt his head being positioned in the guillotine and waited for the proverbial ax to fall.

"I know what's been going on around here," Martin said.

There it was, cutting through his neck in one smooth slice.

"Grace doesn't miss much," Martin went on, "and she's filled me in on everything that's happened while I was away."

"I see," Ryan murmured.

Martin sighed. "I liked you when I hired you, Ryan. I thought you had a good head on your shoulders and you struck me as a man who knew what he wanted. You seemed dedicated to making a place for yourself here at Schuster Systems."

Martin paused to take a drink of coffee then, creating a gut-wrenching pause.

Come on already. Get it over with.

"And I can see now," Martin went on, "that I made a great decision."

A large smile unfurled on Martin's face as Ryan's jaw dropped. What the hell…? "You did?"

"Now, don't be modest. Grace told me how hard you've been working. Staying late some nights, arriving early, coming in on the weekends. And your progress report on the Two Sisters Pub system is impressive. You've gotten twice as far as I'd anticipated, and at this rate we'll bring the project in way under budget—which is good, since I gave Penny a little price break." He winked. "I don't know if she mentioned it or not, but she and I are…close."

Not as close as she and I are. Ryan managed not to say that, and instead felt himself sitting there just nodding like a madman—finally forming the more sensible reply of, "She mentioned it."

"Well, anyway, I just wanted to commend you on the good work you did while I was away. I'm glad to have such a team player on board. But hey," he said, grinning and shaking a finger as Ryan got to his feet, "don't work *too* hard now. You know what they say about all work and no play."

Oh yeah, he knew—but no way was he going to enlighten Martin on just how *much* play he'd combined with work lately, or that he'd definitely not been a dull boy in Martin's absence. "Uh, not to worry," was the only answer he could muster. "And…thanks," he added, backing toward the doorway.

He left the corner office dumbfounded. What the hell had just happened in there? Grace hadn't told Martin about him and Penny? He almost wanted to go back and ask, just to make sure he'd hadn't missed something, because it didn't make sense.

As he headed back down the hall, he looked up to see Grace herself approaching, a stack of papers in her hand, likely heading to the copier. "Grace," he said sharply, stopping her in her tracks and meeting her eyes. Then he spoke more softly. "Thanks. For what you told Martin. And…for what you *didn't* tell him."

She didn't quite smile, but gave him a thoughtful nod that at least seemed to say she didn't think he was pond scum. "I only told him the truth about your work. As for the rest, I figure that's between him and Penny."

"Well, this job means a lot to me, and I appreciate it."

By the time he sat back down behind his own desk, though, his emotions were roiling. Sure, it was great that

Grace hadn't tattled on them, and nice to know she'd noticed the good work he'd done while Martin was away, as well—but the same old issues still remained, just still secret and unspoken.

And the more Ryan thought about it, the more he realized it had almost been a relief of sorts when he'd thought Martin knew the truth. Not that he wanted to lose his job. Of course he didn't. But...he just wanted Penny, damn it! He didn't want to give her up. Not for anything.

And the more he examined it, the less he bought her "we're in different places right now" speech. After all, how could he have misread her so drastically? Those moments when everything had stopped and she'd just clung to him? The way they'd connected on every level? Just because she'd let her wild side out with him didn't mean she didn't want more than just sex. Didn't *feel* more than just sex.

He wasn't a hundred percent sure—he wasn't a hundred percent sure of *anything* today—yet he simply couldn't believe he mattered to her so little. Naturally, the confrontation with Grace yesterday had jarred her, and he could respect her concern over Martin's feelings, but he just didn't believe she was any happier about being apart than he was.

And there was something he could do about this. The notion had been flitting around the edges of his mind for days, but it only materialized into something concrete now. It was a drastic, crazy sort of idea, and he didn't even know if it was feasible, if it would work. But when he thought of spending the rest of his life without his Pretty Penny... Hell, what was the point of living if you didn't take some risks every now and then?

PENNY CLEANED glasses as Patti took inventory of the liquor behind the bar—when the pub's door opened and Martin walked in. "Hello there, Penny," he said, his voice filled with the same bold warmth as his smile.

"H-Hi." Her gretting came out sounding strangled. *Great start.*

She glanced to Patti, who had already put down her pencil. "I'll, uh, do some work in the office," she said, scurrying away to leave them alone.

Penny's first instinct was to remain behind the bar, maintain that comfortable distance between them, but she knew that would be cowardly. So she walked out from behind it and let Martin give her a long, rather excruciating hug before they sat down at one of the tables.

She looked into his eyes. *This is it. This is where I break the poor man's heart.* "Drink?" she heard herself ask anyway—clearly some sort of compulsive attempt to delay the inevitable.

He shook his head. "I have coffee upstairs. And I... really think we should talk, don't you?"

Yes, she did. So Penny took a deep breath and began, nervously. "I've been...worried. Where were you?"

"I'm so sorry, Penny," he apologized, as she'd known he would. "As I said in my phone message, time got away from me out in Vegas."

"I know," she said, nodding. "You were working, learning, soaking up every bit of your conference."

Yet that made his nose scrunch up slightly, his expression shifting into something uncertain. "Well, not exactly. At first, that was the case, but then..."

But then? She raised her eyebrows. "What?"

Martin reached across the table, took her hand in his, and let out a sigh. "Penny, I have something to tell you."

Okay, enough. She couldn't suffer through the slow

pace of this conversation a second longer. She'd been waiting for a week to turn down his proposal, and she had to do it *now*. "I have something to tell you, too, Martin," she said hurriedly, although she tried very hard to sound sad at the same time.

"No, wait." He held up one hand, dropping hers in the process. "Let me go first. I need to get this off my chest."

The protest left her stunned. Martin had something to get off his chest? What the heck could it be? That Mr. Straight and Narrow had over-indulged in a too reasonably priced buffet? That he'd imbibed too many free drinks and lost twenty dollars at blackjack?

"While I was in Vegas, Penny," he said, "I made a big discovery about myself."

She blinked. "What's that?"

"I just don't think…that I'm ready to get married."

Penny's jaw dropped and her heart nearly stopped from the shock. "Oh?"

"I'm so, so sorry, Penny," he said, giving his head a sympathetic tilt, "but when I asked you to marry me, I'm afraid I was…on the rebound from Erica. You remember hearing me talk about Erica, don't you?"

Martin's old girlfriend. "Yes," she said, too bewildered to utter more.

"Well, Erica's in software, too—I don't know if I ever mentioned that. She moved to Minneapolis for a job, which is why we broke up. And to my great surprise, I ran into her at the conference and…"

As Penny's shock slowly wore off, though, it all started to become clear, warming her heart. She gave him a smile. "You realized you couldn't live without her."

"No," Martin said.

Penny let her eyes widen. "No?"

"I realized that…well, that she'd held me back, turned

me into a real stick in the mud." His eyes glazed over slightly. "She was the most conservative woman I've ever met. She didn't like going out, she *hated* parties, all she ever wanted to talk about was work, and she somehow convinced me that I was just like her. She even talked me into wearing matching Christmas sweaters, Penny! It seemed fine at the time because I was in love, but no more." She'd never heard him sound more vehement. "What I discovered in Vegas after sharing a buffet with her and then, on the way back to my hotel, chancing to meet a lovely showgirl named Cherise, is I haven't yet lived."

Penny went numb. "You haven't?"

"Cherise changed the way I look at life. We painted the town red, and lost a thousand dollars at roulette!"

He laughed and Penny gasped.

"We danced the night away in nightclubs!"

Penny gasped again because she'd seen Martin dance and it wasn't pretty.

"We drove out into the desert and made passionate—" He stopped then, his face turning red. "Oh, Penny, I'm so sorry. I'm saying too much." He shook his head in distress. "Look at me—I came home wanting to break this to you gently and instead I just spew it all out like the volcano at the Mirage. Have you seen it, by the way?"

Penny remained nonplussed. "On TV."

"Quite a sight, especially after a few shots of tequila, let me tell you." He stopped again, shaking his head once more, clearly trying to focus on the matter at hand. "What it comes down to, Penny, is…"

She gently tilted her head as her shock slowly gave way to a different sort of understanding this time, one that hit a little closer to home. "You've discovered that you have a wild side," she said softly.

Martin nodded and turned somber. "I'm sorry. This

isn't what I expected or intended when I proposed to you. I hope you're not too hurt."

"Actually, Martin, I…think it's for the best."

His countenance brightened, leaving him to look surprised at how easy this had been, since he'd expected to leave her heartbroken. "Well, thank you for being so understanding. I think the world of you, and I hope we can still be friends."

"Of course," she told him, sealing the promise with a smile.

"And maybe occasionally take in an exhibit at the art museum together?"

"If you won't find it too tame and boring," she teased.

He chuckled in reply, and they both stood up, Martin reaching to squeeze her hand once more. She was watching him walk toward the pub's door—when he stopped and looked back. "I can't believe I'm so rude. What was it you wanted to tell me?"

Oh. That. Penny just shook her head. "Nothing."

"Are you sure?" He leaned slightly forward, as if prodding her.

"Yes, Martin. I'm sure." No need to hurt his feelings—no need at all.

"Well then," he said slowly, "I'll see you soon." Then he turned to go again, leaving her standing in the pub alone.

She stared after him for a long moment, still trying to absorb all he'd just told her. She spent a few seconds thinking about what might've happened if Martin *had* gotten her note that day and joined her in the limo. Thank goodness *Cherise* had been the one to uncover *his* wild side.

Finally, she let out a laugh, but a moment later it dissipated into thoughts of Ryan. She was so happy that *he* had been the man to get in that car with her, and that she'd had the last week and a half with him.

She'd almost considered stopping Martin on his way out, spewing her own truth, about her and Ryan—considering this new change in Martin, he might've thought it was fine, maybe even laughed about their parallel indiscretions. And the horrible guilt she'd been suffering on Martin's behalf had suddenly dissolved into nothing. But she'd decided against it just as quickly as the thought had come—because she still didn't really know how he would take it, and what if she were wrong and it made him angry, or hurt? She still couldn't risk Ryan's job that way.

And yet, maybe, just maybe...did this mean there was hope now for her to share a future with Ryan?

But...no. Depression whisked down through her, squelching that thin ray of hope.

She kept forgetting one important thing. Ryan didn't love her. And how torturous would it be to keep falling deeper and deeper in love with him if he didn't feel the same way? It was a recipe for disaster. And when all was said and done, what they'd shared boiled down to the dreaded F-word—*fling*. There had never been any question about that except maybe in her own lovestruck mind.

Just then, the office door squeaked open a crack, and one of Patti's eyes peered through.

"It's safe," Penny said. "He's gone."

Her sister yanked open the door. "Well? How'd he take it? Tell me everything. Spare no detail."

"You won't believe it."

"Try me," Patti said. "You've shocked me so much lately that it would take quite a whopper to throw me at this point."

"Well, you'd better sit down."

RYAN LINGERED in the shadow of a potted ficus tree in the lobby outside the Two Sisters Pub, watching as Martin exited. He'd been on his way to see Penny, to tell her his crazy idea, when he'd realized Martin had beat him to her. Now he started casually toward the pub again, passing Martin on the way.

"Hey there, Ryan, scouting for a little breakfast?"

Hmm—the guy still seemed awfully happy for someone who'd just been dumped.

Unless—oh God—he *hadn't* been. Had Penny somehow given him a different answer than she'd told Ryan she would. The thought nearly paralyzed him, but he kept the reaction inside. "Uh, yeah."

"Great danishes at Penny's place." Martin pointed, then winked at Ryan for the second time in half an hour. "She gets a fresh tray from the bakery across the street every morning."

Martin moved on toward the elevators, and Ryan picked up his pace until he practically burst through the pub's door. Penny and her sister sat at one of the tables, and both looked up, clearly stunned to see him barreling into their restaurant.

Patti sighed. "I'll be in the back," she said, then rose to make her way to the office.

Ryan wasted no time striding to the table, staring down at the woman he loved. "Did you tell him you wouldn't marry him? Did you?"

"Not exactly, but—"

Damn it, it was just as he'd feared. "Penny, you can't marry him! You don't love him! And he didn't even call you for over a week! What kind of stand-up guy does that?

The answer is—none, and you deserve a stand-up guy. I won't let you throw away your whole—"

"Wait!" she interrupted, getting to her feet. "If you'd let me finish, you'd know the only reason I didn't tell him was because he told me first. He doesn't want to marry me, either."

The news nearly knocked the wind out of Ryan. "Is he nuts?"

"Well, he *did* seem a bit out of sorts, but—"

"Listen," he cut her off again. "I have something to say and I can't go slow or I might start thinking I'm crazy and stop."

She tilted her head, her pretty eyes wide upon him. "Well then, go ahead."

"I'm gonna quit my job and start my own company," he announced.

She looked confused. "Why?"

But he thought the answer was obvious. "So I can be with you. So we can do wild things if we want to and it won't be anyone else's business. And because…" he spoke more softly now, "…I can't sleep nights without you."

He saw her pull in a deep breath and said a silent prayer. *Please tell me you want me, too.*

"Is this," she began uncertainly, "what you really want?"

"To start my own company?" he replied. "Well…not exactly." He shifted his weight from one foot to the other. "I mean, I like it where I am. I like the work I'm doing for Martin and I already know he values it. I think I could go places at Schuster, grow with the company." Then he tilted his head, bent one finger to lift her chin, and gazed into those warm blue eyes that had the power to swallow him. "But do I want to be with you? Absolutely. Without a doubt. All the time. Otherwise, I'd never even consider this."

Penny's heart skipped a beat. She couldn't believe Ryan would make that kind of sacrifice, take that kind of risk, for her. She'd never been more touched by any gesture in her life, but she couldn't let him do something like that for her. She pressed her hands to his chest. "Ryan, it might not be necessary to take such drastic steps for us to be together."

"What do you mean?"

"Didn't you hear what I said about Martin? He doesn't want to marry me. And when he was out in Vegas, he wasn't just working."

Ryan arched one brow. "What was he doing?"

She smiled into his eyes and spoke softly. "He was finding his wild side."

Ryan blinked. "You're kidding."

"He met a showgirl. Cherise."

"Cherise?"

"I think they had sex in the desert. And drank a lot of tequila."

Now both brows rose—in clear disbelief. And maybe a hint of admiration. "Way to go, Marty." Then his eyes took on the sexy look she loved. "And you know, that sounds kinda fun—like something you and I should try."

She laughed. "The desert or the tequila?"

"Nothing against a good shot of tequila, but I was definitely talking about the desert."

She smiled her agreement, leaning in to lift a slow, sweet kiss to his lips. "I didn't tell Martin about us," she went on. "I still didn't know how he might feel about it. And I couldn't risk your job that way without discussing it with you first. But maybe what I did while he was away, and what you and I choose to do now, won't matter anymore. Maybe if we told him the truth, he would understand."

The same conviction had already hit Ryan, even before she'd suggested it, and he knew what he had to do. He supposed the answer had been dangling in front of him all along, but he'd been too afraid to reach out and grab it.

"I'll be back in a few minutes," he told Penny.

She tilted her head. "You're going to do this now, tell him this very minute? I mean, shouldn't we talk about this first, come up with a plan?"

"Just trust me," he said.

———

FIVE MINUTES LATER, Ryan stood before Martin's desk. He wasn't going to beat around the bush. He'd waffled on this for too long in the first place and was ready to take action. He needed to clear the air and quit keeping secrets. He needed to be the sort of man Penny deserved. A stand-up guy, just like he'd told her. "Martin, there's something you need to know."

His boss smiled, and it finally occurred to Ryan what he was *really* smiling about. Cherise. In the desert. "What's that?" Martin asked.

"I don't know how else to say this, except plainly. While you were away, I fell in love with Penny."

Martin quit smiling and leaned forward in his chair, as if he couldn't quite fathom what he was hearing.

"I realize I was overstepping," Ryan went on, "but it was...bigger than the both of us. I never really knew what it meant when people said that, but now I do. I tried not to want her, but"—he shook his head—"I can't help it. I can't stop it. So...is there any chance this is okay with you or, all things considered, should I just go clean out my desk?"

Martin tilted his head first to one side, then the other. "Let me get this straight. While I was away, you fell for Penny."

"Yeah." Ryan nodded.

And Martin leaned further over his desk. "*My* Penny."

Ryan thought the point arguable now, but instead just said, "That's the one."

"So you're saying while *I* was out in Vegas, *you* were here romancing the woman I had just proposed to?"

To say the very least. But he kept it simple. "Yep."

He tensed as Martin took a deep breath, slowly let it back out—and then flashed a smile so bold it made Ryan flinch. "Well, that's the best damn news I've heard all day! Other than her not hating me for withdrawing my proposal, that is. It killed me to hurt her like that—she's a tenderhearted woman, you know."

"I…I know." He left it at that.

"And she's…well, she's very conservative. Very innocent. Pure at heart."

Ryan held in his smile and simply nodded.

"So nothing would please me more than to see Penny with a great guy like you, Ryan. I hope you'll make her very happy."

Oh yeah. I'll make her happy, all right.

———

PENNY HAD SPENT the last half an hour trying to absorb all that happened this morning; heck, in the whole past two weeks. Martin didn't love her, and had likely *never* loved her —he'd merely been on the rebound. And Ryan really cared for her. Enough to risk the career that was so precious to him, and so important to his family. And in the midst of wrapping her head around all that, she'd also spent time worrying about Martin's reaction and praying Ryan's career remained intact. It was difficult to start a business—she knew that from experience—and she wanted Ryan to be happy with his decision. So much remained at stake; her heart turned somersaults in her chest.

She'd just finished updating Patti when the pub's door flew open. Penny almost dropped a beer mug—then her eyes desperately searched Ryan's as he bounded toward her.

Patti instantly pivoted toward the door that led to the street. "I'll go take a walk."

Penny smiled her apology—poor Patti, always having to make herself scarce these days due to all the drama in her sister's life—and then she shifted her attention back to the man she loved, biting her lip as he neared the bar. "Well?"

"He's glad—he gives us his blessing" Ryan said, smiling. "Although it wouldn't have mattered. Either way, I'd be down here right now telling you I love you."

Penny caught her breath. He loved her? He loved her.

Pure, wild happiness like none she'd ever known soared through her veins.

But then confusion warred with her elation. "But I thought…I thought this was just a fling. I thought you couldn't fall in love that fast. Remember, you told me that once."

He took her hands in his and gazed deeply into her eyes. "I was wrong, honey. And I was a fool to think anything was more important than the way I want you. I love you like crazy, Penny Halloran, and I don't care who knows it anymore. In fact, I intend to spread the news far and wide." Her whole body went warm as he pulled her into his embrace, and as he kissed her, long and deep, it came with the comfort of knowing this was just the beginning for them. The beginning of kisses, but also the beginning of so much more.

When finally he pulled back, it was to cast one of his classic wicked looks, she felt it between her thighs. "So tell me, do you have any other fantasies we haven't explored yet?"

She lowered her chin and let the desire that no longer embarrassed her show in her gaze. "I do, in fact."

"Don't keep me in suspense."

"Well…I've always kind of wanted to do it here, on the bar." She pointed.

He peered at the restaurant's long mahogany showpiece, then glanced over her shoulder toward the downtown city street just outside. "Kinda risky with all these plate glass windows. Are you ready to go that far?"

She didn't answer, but her body flared with the familiar heat he inspired in her and she kissed him again, this time plundering his warm mouth with her tongue. Their bodies pressed together, thighs intertwining, and she'd just begun to lose herself in the sweet friction when Ryan whispered breathlessly in her ear. "I, uh, hate to break it to you, but even *I'm* not that wild."

He gazed past her again, first toward the street, then to the pub's office. "We should look into getting some big shades for these windows, but for now, honey, we'll have to make due in there."

At the moment, Penny hardly cared *where* they did it, as long as she had her way with him, *now*. Although a slow smile spread across her face as she realized she finally had what she'd always dreamed of—the kind of passion that was too urgent to wait. Grabbing Ryan's tie, she led him into the office and shut the door.

About the Author

Toni Blake's love of writing began when she won an essay contest in the fifth grade. Soon after, she penned her first novel, nineteen notebook pages long. Since then, Toni has become a RITA™-nominated author of more than twenty contemporary romance novels, her books have received the National Readers Choice Award and Bookseller's Best Award, and her work has been excerpted in *Cosmo*. Toni lives in the Midwest and enjoys traveling, crafts, and spending time outdoors.

Learn more about Toni and her books at:
www.toniblake.com

facebook.com/AuthorToniBlake

twitter.com/AuthorToniBlake

instagram.com/AuthorToniBlake

Look for these other classic Toni Blake reissues

The Cinderella Scheme

The Guy Next Door

The Bewitching Hour

The Weekend Wife

Also by Toni Blake

The Rose Brothers Trilogy

Brushstrokes

Mistletoe

Heartstrings

The Coral Cove Series

All I Want is You

Love Me If You Dare

Take Me All the Way

The Destiny Series

One Reckless Summer

Sugar Creek

Whisper Falls

Holly Lane

Willow Springs

Half Moon Hill

Christmas in Destiny

Wildest Dreams

The Red Diary

Letters to a Secret Lover

Tempt Me Tonight

Swept Away

Made in the USA
Middletown, DE
08 December 2018